MW01222853

A CANDLE IN THE WIND

A NOVEL

VANESSA ORIVOLO

A Candle in the Wind

By Vanessa Orivolo

Cover design by Clint Botha

Edited by Todd Foley

TABLE OF CONTENTS

For Mom, for telling me to write it down.

For Mel. May you find your happy ending.

Fall

1.

It started on the first day of school. I was sitting in my homeroom, and felt that uncomfortable feeling you get when you know someone is watching you. I shifted around a little in my seat and glanced around the room trying to be discreet. It's hard enough being the new girl in school without everyone in your first class of the day thinking you're stalking them.

Then I saw him. I could tell he was tall even though he was sitting down; his legs were stretched long beyond his desk and the desk in front of him. He had bronze coloured skin and shaggy blond hair that almost fell in front of his eyes. The bluest eyes I had ever seen were staring at me. I turned back around and tried not to wonder why one of the best looking guys I had ever seen was looking – better yet, gaping – at me as if I had just turned the entire classroom to gold.

The rest of the day passed quickly and I forgot all about the dream boy from homeroom. I started my walk home from school and began to dream about all the things I would be doing if I were back home again. Home being Toronto, where I, Aria Brooks, was supposed to be starting my last year of high school – not here in Jordan Falls, a small town outside of Vancouver to where my mother had decided to move me, herself and my sister Quinn.

Yup, that's right. My mother had decided that it was logical to move me to the other side of the country all because she had met the so-called "new" love of her life.

Robert "Just Call Me Rob" McDermott was Mom's new husband (I still cringe saying the words). Robert was a psychologist who had met Mom – also a psychologist – working on a special case study last year. Might I add that it was only six months after my father had passed away; apparently there was no shame there. Mom had just jumped on the dating band wagon like she hadn't been married to another man for 25 years and here we are.

My senior year was supposed to be it for me; it was supposed to be *the* year. I was captain of the basketball team, senior class president. I had an amazing family, a great life and the best friends a girl could ask for. Now I was stuck in Jordan Falls, with no friends, no boyfriend and, oh, a new dad. This was all looking pretty peachy.

I stopped walking when I reached our new house. It was a nice house, I'll give you that. An old two-story white Victorian mansion, with a driveway leading to steep stairs and a large porch that wrapped all the way to the back of the house. It was a beauty. I'd dreamed about living in a house like this back in Toronto where our Tudor style home had been sufficient for years. I made my way down our long driveway and let myself inside.

"Hello?" I called into the empty foyer.

"Aria" a voice called from the kitchen. "That you?"

I followed the voice into the kitchen where my older sister Quinn was chopping some vegetables on a cutting board.

"How's it going?" I asked, tossing my book bag by the door.

"Good. Just enjoying my last day of freedom." Quinn was starting her first year as an intern for medical school tomorrow. She had transferred to be closer to Mom and myself, as well as her boyfriend Jeremy who was a doctor working in Jordan Falls. Jordan Falls University was known for its Science and Medicine program. Jordan Falls Hospital (JFH) was also one of the top 10 trauma hospitals in Canada. Quinn had been stoked to find out Mom was planning a move here.

"Lucky you," I grabbed a carrot from the cutting board and popped it into my mouth.

"How was school?" Quinn asked me.

"Oh you know," I replied, "Same old. 10 minutes a class, got the course outline, got a big lecture about how this was the year that mattered for my future."

"Doesn't sound like much has changed since I graduated,"

"Guess not."

"Meet any new people?"

"Not really," I told her. "Probably tomorrow. Is Mom home?"

"In her office," Quinn said. "She said she wanted to see you when you got home." Fantastic. Mom's office (Robert's as well) was outside in the backyard above the garage. Most of her work was spent doing psych evaluations and counselling that took place at the hospital, but she often did private counselling as well. Robert had insisted that we find a house where both of them would have enough space to do their work. What a gem.

3

I headed out the back door and across the yard to Mom's office. I took the back stairs two at a time and knocked on the back door.

"Come in," I heard Mom call from the other side of the door. I opened the door and walked in. "Hi, sweetie." Mom looked up from her computer screen and smiled at me. "How was your first day of school?"

"Oh you know," I muttered. "It was...school...different building, different kids, same general concept."

"Make any new friends?" she asked. The one great thing about having a mother who's a psychologist is getting the third degree about everything.

"Oh yeah," I replied, my voice thick with sarcasm. "I'm pretty sure by tomorrow I will be the new queen of Jordan Falls High." Mom raised her eyebrows at me. "Anyways, Mom, I was just going to go play some ball in the driveway before dinner. Can we talk more after?"

The key to leaving a conversation with Mom is always leaving the topic of discussion open for more. Plan achieved. Mom's eyes were already planted back on her computer screen.

"Sure, honey," she said. "I'll see you at dinner." With that as my cue, I bolted from her office and back to the house. I threw on my running gear, grabbed my basketball and went out to the new hoop Robert had put up for me in the driveway. Basketball try outs were in two weeks and I was determined to make the team. I wasn't sure how big basketball was in Jordan Falls or if their team was even one worth trying out for, but needless to say I needed to keep my options open.

I started throwing some free throws when I heard a voice from behind me. "Hey, you go to Jordan right?" I tried to push aside the sarcastic remark to this question. Seeing as there was only one high school in Jordan Falls, the question wasn't exactly one that involved rocket science.

I turned around. In front of me stood a pretty girl about my age. She had long wavy dark hair, bright blue eyes and a smile that looked like she had just stepped out of a magazine.

"Just started today," I said. She held out her hands for the basketball; I tossed it to her. She shot a solid three pointer, nothing but net. "Nice shot," I told her.

"Thanks," she smiled, "I'm Callie. Callie Jeakins."

"Aria Brooks."

"I live next door," she said, pointing to the massive house next to mine. "Where are you from?"

"Toronto," I bounced the basketball. "My mom just remarried, so we moved here last week."

"What do you think so far?"

I bit my lip. "Well, it's – quiet?" I fumbled for lack of a better word, but Callie just laughed.

"It's a lot to get used to if you're from the big city, that's for sure."

I'd say it's a lot to not get used to, but I wasn't going to share my opinion with her.

"I grew up in the city," she explained. "We lived in Edmonton until my first year of high school."

"Lucky you."

"It's not so bad," Callie said as she grabbed the basketball out of my hands and ran to the hoop for a layup. "You'll get used to it. The first month is always the hardest."

"I'll remember that," I said dryly and smiled at her.

"So are you going out for varsity?" she asked, motioning towards the basketball.

"That's the plan. You play I take it?"

"About as often as I breathe oxygen," she smiled at me. "I'm the team captain."

"Nice. I was my team captain back at home." She passed me the ball.

"Maybe we can co-captain," she offered. "I know what it's like being the new kid in town. Especially in your senior year, that's rough." I shot the ball, and it went in. "Besides," she continued, "you've got a pretty mean jump shot." I smiled at her.

Callie and I played basketball for the next hour. By the end of our game, I was starting to feel a little less tense. It seemed there was a sign of normal life in Jordan Falls after all.

At dinner that night, I did my best to be pleasant. It was hard to be around Robert; even harder to be around Mom and Robert together. When Dad died, I didn't know how anything would ever be normal again.

Dad had been a great man. A man of character, integrity. A man who would do anything for his family. Dad was the one who had taught me my first jump shot, taken me to my first basketball game, driven me to every tryout. He had died of a heart attack. The man had had perfect health all his life and two days before Christmas went to take the garbage out and fell down on the driveway. It was strange starting off somewhere new without him.

Part of me was angry at Mom for marrying Robert so quickly – she couldn't just replace Dad. Another part of me, a more grown-up part, understood that after being with someone for as long as she had been with Dad, it must be hard not to have someone around all the time. I didn't side with that particular part often.

The first few months had been the hardest. First there was Mom who tried to counsel us all with her Ph.D in psychology. There was no suppressing our emotions allowed.

Next was Quinn, the ever so perfect daughter who always put on a happy face for everyone. It was hard living up to an older sister like her. Quinn had always been the brain of the family, where I was more the jock and the brat with the attitude. We were seven years apart in age which put us at different ends of the spectrum growing up, but we were a lot closer now.

Then there was me. After Dad's death, part of me felt almost frozen, like I was just going through the motions. I still remember the day Mom introduced Robert to us. I didn't speak to her for a whole week. Don't get me wrong, I don't have anything against Robert; he just wasn't my dad. He kept insisting I called him Rob, but Robert felt more suiting. He was a tall, burly, intimidating man. He had dark brown hair and dark pools of ink for eyes. Whenever he asked you a question, it always felt as though he was interrogating you without believing your answers. Quinn always told me I was exaggerating about Robert, but you try having two psychologists as parents! It's like they have a pool going to see who can get the most emotion out of you.

After dinner, Robert had a meeting with a patient, so Mom, Quinn and I were left to clean up the kitchen. My mother is one of those anal people who insisted that every dish be rinsed spotless before putting them in the dishwasher. In my opinion, this defeated the purpose of a dishwasher, but I was wise enough to do as I was told.

As Quinn rinsed, I loaded the dishes into the dishwasher, and Mom began transferring the leftovers into plastic containers and then into the fridge. I watched the two of them at work. Mom, Quinn and I were almost identical as three relatives could be when it came to looks. All slim-figured with blonde hair – although mine was very curly, Mom's had a natural wave and Quinn's was bone straight – and matching green eyes and cheek bones. People often had mistaken Mom for our older sister; she was in pretty lean shape for 45.

I listened to Mom and Quinn chat about their work at the hospital and how that nice lady from down the road had brought over a casserole to welcome us to the neighborhood yesterday. "Weren't people just the nicest things here!" It took everything I had to suppress my eye roll.

After the dishes were done, I went upstairs to my room and reviewed my timetable for the fall semester. First period English, second fitness, third chemistry and fourth history. Not too shabby. I had no idea what I was planning on doing after high school. I wasn't an overachiever like Quinn and I definitely didn't want to spend my life talking to people about their problems like Mom. Oh well, I still had the whole year to figure it out. I did however know one thing for sure: I definitely was not going to stick around Jordan Falls for any longer than absolutely necessary. The city girl in me was not going to turn into a small town girl any time soon.

The next morning my alarm sounded at 6 o'clock a.m. - not a happy morning sound. I hit snooze twice before dragging myself out of bed and into the shower. I am not a morning person. In fact, Mom always joked that I should carry around an IV of caffeine until noon. I showered quickly and scrunched my curly blonde hair – too lazy to be bothered with blow drying or straightening it. I then reviewed my clothing options for the day. I went with layers; it was already getting to be cold for fall. I grabbed my book bag and ran down the stairs where my nose filled with the scent of bacon, eggs and coffee.

Mom, Quinn and Quinn's boyfriend Jeremy were all sitting at the kitchen table. Robert was standing over a frying pan in front of the stove wearing an apron that said "Kiss the Cook" over his crisp black suit.

"Good morning," Robert's voice boomed ever so cheerfully.

"Morning," I muttered, walking over to the table and sitting down.

"Coffee?" Mom asked as she started filling up my mug.

"Please," I said eagerly.

"Aria would never turn down coffee," Quinn teased and everyone laughed. I sipped my coffee like it was the first time I had ever tasted the wonderful invention.

"How would you like your eggs, Aria?" Robert asked me.

"I'll just grab a bagel," I told him. After seeing both Mom's and Quinn's disapproving frowns, I spoke again, "Thanks, though."

"No problem," he said.

"You should really eat a balanced breakfast," Mom said. I chugged the rest of my coffee and grabbed a bagel from the middle of the table.

"Don't worry, Mom." I waved the bagel in the air. "I've got it covered. I better get going, don't want to be late." I zipped out of the kitchen before anyone could say a word. On my walk down the driveway I ran into Callie waiting for me at the end.

"Hey," she said, smiling at me. "I thought you might want to walk to school together?"

"Sounds good." I took a bite of my bagel.

On our way to school Callie filled me in on the goings on at Jordan Falls High School and basically gave a short review of her life story. Callie had moved to Jordan Falls when she was 12. She was an only child and her parents had moved her here to open up a restaurant/coffee shop called Jay's. I had been there once with Quinn when we first arrived in Jordan Falls; it was basically your average restaurant. Callie worked there on weekends and when she wasn't playing basketball which she was counting on getting a scholarship for. Apparently Jordan Falls' basketball was more competitive than I thought.

By the time we got to school I knew as much about Callie and her life as I probably ever needed to know. Man, could this chick talk. It was nice to have someone to talk to, though.

Callie followed me to my locker; hers was just a few lockers down. We compared our schedules. We had our first three classes together. I was pulling my books out of my locker when I noticed Callie staring down the hallway.

"What's up?" I asked, following her gaze.

"Logan." Callie's eyes looked fierce and her jaw was clenched. I watched a tall, built boy taking textbooks out of his locker. He had jet black hair, pale skin and was dressed in all black.

"Who's that?" I asked. "The school mime?"

Callie looked like I had just kicked her in the stomach. "Logan's my ex boyfriend."

"Oh." I chewed on my bottom lip, unsure of what she wanted me to say. Callie slammed her locker shut and grabbed my arm, dragging me down the opposite way of the hall from Logan. "Are you okay?" I found some words this time.

"He just –," Callie stopped her sentence, looking frazzled. "He just," she tried again. "He makes me so mad."

"Because…?" That came out a little more impatiently than intended.

"Logan and I started dating a really long time ago," Callie explained. "I've known Logan since we were in diapers; our parents are old friends." I continued to listen. "Last summer, everything changed between Logan and me. He had just gotten his driver's license and was driving his little brother Jamie home from swimming lessons one

11

morning. The car got t-boned by another driver who was texting. Logan wasn't hurt, but Jamie ended up in a wheelchair, paralyzed from the waist down."

"That's awful," I said, feeling an instant pang of remorse for Logan.

"Logan blames himself for what happened to Jamie," Callie frowned. "He changed a lot. He stopped coming out with everyone, he was moody and introverted. And the black clothes…it's ridiculous."

"What about them?" I was curious.

"He didn't used to look like that," she explained. "He's going through something. He won't even talk to me. One day he just stopped answering my calls and wouldn't talk to me, period." Her eyes were wet and she looked away from me to regain composure.

"What a jackass," I said, putting a hand on her arm.

"He's not," she said defensively. "He didn't used to be this way. He just took it really hard."

"You still don't deserve to be treated like that," I pointed out.

"I guess."

Callie sighed and the bell rang. "We're late," she said, scrunching up her lips in annoyance, "we better get moving." I followed her down the hall.

First period English was pretty basic. We were going to be reading *The Catcher in the Rye*, a book I had already read in last year's English class. A few lectures and homework assignments later and it was lunch time. Callie and I stopped off at our lockers and then she took me to the cafeteria. We walked over to a big table by one of the windows that looked outside onto the track.

"Aria, this is everyone," Callie said, "Everyone, this is Aria." So much for introductions.

"Everyone," as I learned over the next few minutes, consisted of Lauren and Amy, two girls from the basketball team, and Scott and Connor, from the baseball team. As I sat with them, I saw that Connor was obviously interested in Callie. Callie's eyes, of course, seemed to be somewhere else. I took a bite out of my peanut butter and jelly sandwich when I heard Connor call out across the cafeteria to someone.

"Hey Lawson!" he shouted. "Over here!" I looked up from my sandwich and saw the blond beauty from homeroom walking over to our table, staring at me. I took another bite and focused on chewing. I heard Callie's voice.

"Aria this is-".

"Matt." He sat down across from me and gave me the biggest smile I had ever seen in my entire life. "Matt Lawson. Nice to meet you, Aria." He grinned again.

"Hi." I said and almost groaned at my lame reply. He kept smiling.

"Matt used to be Logan's best friend," Callie whispered to me. I nodded, taking another bite of my sandwich.

"Peanut butter and jelly," Matt said, "My favourite."

The rest of lunch was pretty normal. I got to know everyone a little better at the table. I also noticed that

13

Matt's eyes did not leave me the entire lunch period. As Callie and I walked to chemistry, she made a comment that sparked my interest a bit.

"Matt thinks you're cute," she told me, smiling.

"Really?" I asked, trying to keep my tone even. "How can you tell?"

"Well for one thing, he was looking at you like you were the only girl in the room. I've known Matt along time and I've never seen him look at a girl like that."

"He doesn't have a girlfriend?" I asked casually.

"He dates a little, but he's never been with anyone long term."

"Plays the field?" I asked, holding my breath.

"Nope. That's not Matt. Just a guy who knows what he wants and hasn't found it yet." I let my breath out and it made a small "whoosh" sound.

"Interesting," I said. Callie laughed.

"Come on. We can't be late for chem lab."

After 75 minutes of torturous chemistry, my brain was about ready to explode. I do not have a science brain; that's all Quinn in our family. Needless to say, I was very excited to have history as my last class of the day. Callie and I went our separate ways as I went to history and she went to French – a language that I had decided not to pursue this year. I picked out a seat in the middle of the room and tried my best to blend in.

"Hey." I heard a voice from behind me. Matt's voice. I spun around just as he slid into the seat behind me, stretching out his long legs past my desk.

"Hi," I said. "Looks like we have history together." Way to state the obvious, Aria. I felt my mouth go dry and wet my lips.

"Looks that way." He smiled that wide grin again. "So, you're from Toronto?"

"Yeah. Just moved here last week."

"And how do you like the lovely Jordan Falls so far?"

"It's nice."

He laughed, "You hate it."

I bit my lip. "No, I don't –" I started, but he cut me off.

"It's okay. I can't wait to get out of this place next year."

"Oh yeah? And where are you going?"

"Anywhere that has snow and where I can play baseball." He smiled at me, his blue eyes twinkling.

"Baseball in the snow?" I cringed.

He laughed. "Baseball in the spring, snowboarding in the winter. My two true loves. Do you board?"

"I used to ski, but haven't boarded much." The bell rang and our teacher walked into the room and began taking attendance. I turned back around to face the front of the room.

"I'll have to teach you sometime," Matt's voice whispered in my ear, making the hairs on my neck stand up straight. I just nodded.

After class Matt walked me to my locker, "Can I give you a ride home?" he asked me. I hesitated. "I've had my license for over a year." He put his hand over his heart. "Scout's honour."

I laughed.

"Okay, why not."

We walked to Matt's locker together, and then outside to the school parking lot where he led me to a shiny black pick-up truck. He walked around and opened the passenger door for me. I climbed in. Once he started the engine, an old Beatles song blared through the speakers and I sang along.

"You a Beatles fan?" he asked.

"Love them."

He smiled at me again.

"Hey, you want to go grab a cup of coffee somewhere?"

"Okay. But not for too long. I have homework."

"Homework," Matt said. "Look at you, a keener on day one."

"I figure I might as well earn a good reputation at this place."

He raised his eyebrows at me, "You've had a bad one in the past?"

I gave him a friendly shove on the shoulder. "Dream on!"

We went to Jay's Restaurant in town and Matt ordered us two cups of coffee to go. "I was thinking we could take a walk through the park, if that's okay," he said. "It's just right next door." I nodded.

He led me down to Jordan Falls Provincial Park. It was a large park with trails and grassy areas, as well as a large swimming lake in the middle. We walked down to the lake and sat on the grass.

"So," Matt said casually, "What's your story?"

"My story?" I nervously grabbed a strand of my long blonde hair and began fidgeting with it.

"Yup." He shot me that grin one more time. I had a feeling he had melted the hearts of many girls with that grin. I took a sip of my coffee. "I want to know everything about you, Aria Brooks," he said in a soft voice.

I felt like his deep blue eyes were staring so far inside of me they could see my every thought and desire. That was the moment that I knew that Matt Lawson was not just your ordinary guy. And little did I know, he would change my life forever.

2.

Matt and I had spent the last four hours talking and I had found out everything about Matthew Thomas Lawson. He came from a big family, two parents, and six kids. He was the second oldest and had lived in Jordan Falls all his life. His dad was an elementary school principal and his mom a piano teacher. He loved snowboarding, baseball and working on cars. He, like me, did decently in school. He went to church every Sunday, helped teach Sunday school and volunteered at the senior's home once a month. On paper he was perfect, almost too perfect. He was also extremely easy to talk to and easy going. He didn't say anything about his past relationship with Logan, though; I didn't really feel comfortable inquiring.

We stayed at the lake until the sun began to set. I looked down and saw that my phone had been on silent. Four missed calls. Crap, Mom was going to kill me. It was already past seven.

I jumped up. "I have to go. My mom is going to freak out – she's a tad over protective. You know, new town and stuff."

Matt nodded. "I'm sorry. I'll drive you home."

We got into the car and continued chatting on the short drive home. A few minutes later, Matt pulled into my driveway.

"If you want I can come in and talk to your parents," he offered.

I smiled. "That's okay, I can handle Mom." He was lucky Robert wasn't home though. That would be another story.

"Okay." He got out of the truck and came around to my side of the truck and opened my door. I hopped out. "I had a lot of fun today, Aria."

"Me too." I swung my book bag over my shoulder and looked up at his 6'3 tall frame towering over my 5'7 body. He smiled one more time.

"I'll see you tomorrow then."

"I'll see you." I jogged up the front steps and closed the front door behind me, trying to catch my breath. I walked into the kitchen. Mom was sitting at the table. "Hey, Mom," I said, trying to act as casual as possible.

She narrowed her eyes and looked me up and down, examining me from head to toe. "Out with friends?" she asked.

"Yeah. Friends from school. I met some new people."

"Who's truck?" she asked. Crap. I thought I almost snuck past that one.

"Just a guy from school."

"Does he have a name?"

"Matt," I said, easing up a little. At least she didn't seem mad.

"Just call next time you plan on missing dinner, okay?" She tucked a stray strand of hair behind her right ear.

"Okay." I smiled. She stood up and gave me a quick hug.

"I'll warm up some dinner for you," she said.

"Thanks, Mom." I sat down at the table. "Where's Robert?"

"He's away on business for the next week." Robert was a very high profile psychologist and often travelled to testify in court cases and other things that were of no interest to me. As long as he was out of my way, that was all that mattered.

"I thought the whole point of us moving here was so that he didn't have to travel?"

Mom frowned at me. "He's just finishing up a case." She handed me a plate with some chicken, rice and salad on it. I picked at the food. "I wish you'd focus on your relationship with Robert more."

Here we go.

"Kind of hard to do when he's not around." The words shot out of my mouth before I could think about them.

Mom sat down next to me. "He's a very good man," she said. "I think if you gave him a chance you'd really like him."

"He's not my dad," I said slowly. From the day I had met Robert I felt like he had tried to jump in where he wasn't wanted. He was always badgering me, asking questions and trying to enforce parental rules and boundaries.

Mom sighed, "No one's trying to make him take the place of Dad, sweetheart."

"Right," I glared at her. "You didn't seem to have any trouble bringing him into our family right away." I stopped myself. Mom's face was crestfallen. "I'm sorry," I said. "I didn't mean it like that. I just miss him a lot."

"I miss him too," she said. "Every single day. Your father and I were married for 25 years. He was my high school sweetheart, my first love. Things like that don't just go away. But your father would have wanted us to go on living our lives in memory of him, not sitting around feeling sad all the time."

"I know," I said, taking a deep breath. "I don't want to talk about this. I'm going to go play ball."

Mom looked at me, her eyes flooded with concern. "We're going to have to talk about it one day." I gave her a half smile and walked out of the kitchen, leaving my untouched dinner behind.

I changed into some old sweats, tied up my runners and went out the front door to the driveway. I shot free throw after free throw until I was so tired I felt like my arms couldn't lift anymore. I lay down on the grass and stared up at the stars in the dark sky.

Half an hour had passed when a car pulled into the driveway and I sat up. Quinn's car. She got out and walked over to me. Even in her scrubs after a 12-hour work day, she still looked as gorgeous as ever. She sat down next to me on the lawn.

"How was your first day?" I asked.

"Long," she sighed, "but lots of hands-on experience. It was great."

"Cool."

Quinn studied my face carefully. "Mom told me about your fight."

"It wasn't a fight, and how the heck did you hear about that? You haven't even been in the house." I scowled.

"This new fangled invention called cell phones," Quinn replied sarcastically. "You okay?"

I sighed. "I want to like Robert. I do." I knew I was lying as I said this, but I didn't care right now. "I just miss him a lot, Quinn."

Quinn put her arm around me. "So do I. But Mom's happy so we should be happy for her, as hard as it is. And I know Mom misses him too."

I stood up and bounced the basketball. "I know I shouldn't give her such a hard time."

Quinn grabbed the ball from my hands and shot the ball. It went in. Go figure, the girl had never played a day of ball in her life. She hugged me.

"No you shouldn't, but it happens." She smiled at me and ruffled my hair lightly. "Come on, let's go inside." I followed her up the front steps. "So tell me about this Matt character." Her eyes twinkled as she opened the front door. I groaned and rolled my eyes as she closed the door behind us.

3.

The next morning I walked out the front door and into Callie, who was standing on my front porch.

"Hey," I said. "How's it -"

"Don't hey me!" Callie grabbed my arm and steered me down the front steps. "I heard that you went out with Matt after school yesterday. Details!" For someone who I had only known for two days, this was one pushy girl.

"We just went down to the lake and had coffee," I said. "And then he drove me home. No big deal. We had history last period and just ended up leaving together."

"No big deal!" Callie exclaimed. "Right!" I laughed in response, unsure of what else she wanted me to say. I'd just met the guy; it's not like I was going to start planning our wedding.

"Look," I told her. "I'm new here. I'm not really looking for anything other than friendship right now. I'd rather just lay low for a while."

"Whatever you say." Callie gave me a teasing grin and then changed the subject to basketball tryouts the following week. I tried to focus on our conversation but found myself distracted.

School that day seemed to drag on and on. We had a pop quiz in chemistry that I was sure I failed due to my lack of homework the night before. By the time history rolled around I was glad it was Friday and I had the weekend ahead of me to unwind. I took the same seat as yesterday, and sure enough a few minutes later heard a voice behind me.

"Missed you at lunch today." Matt's voice. I turned around to face him.

"Callie and I stayed after fitness class to practice some basketball with some of the girls," I told him.

"Callie's working you hard," he commented. "It's only the third day of school!"

"Yeah, Callie wants the team to win nationals this year, so it's all or nothing. Besides, I still need to make the team so I figure I should get in as much practice with the girls as possible."

Matt smiled at me. "I'm sure you will have no problem making the team."

"Thanks. I guess we'll find out next week."

"Hey, are you going to the bonfire tonight?" Matt asked me. The bonfire. Callie had mentioned this to me yesterday. On the first Friday night of every school year, the senior class always had a huge bonfire down by the lake. It was tradition.

"Maybe." I shrugged and turned around to face the front of the room as the bell rang.

"You should come," Matt whispered. "It'll be fun. It's a great way to meet new people." I shrugged my shoulders again and didn't turn around.

I spent the next hour and a bit trying to focus on the effects of World War I, but I just couldn't. I couldn't stop thinking about Matt. I wasn't the type of girl to fall hard for a guy, especially a guy I had only known for two days and seen a grand total of three times. There was just something about him that scared me half to death and currently I was ready to run in the opposite direction.

As soon as the bell rang signaling the end of the day, I burst full speed out of history toward my locker, grabbed all the textbooks I needed for the weekend and was almost out the front doors when I heard someone call my name. So close. I turned around and saw Callie running towards me.

"What's the hurry?" she asked, stopping in front of me.

"No hurry," I shrugged. "I just want to get home."

"Okay, but I'll see you tonight right?"

I hesitated. "I don't know."

"Come on," she nudged me. "It will be tons of fun. I'll tell you what, I'll come over after dinner and we can get ready and go together."

"Well-"

"No excuses!" she said, cutting me off. "I'll see you later!" And off she went. I shook my head and started my walk home from school.

I let myself into an empty house, which was a relief. I didn't feel like getting drilled about my day or how I was adapting to life in Jordan Falls. I started up on some chemistry equations but promptly gave up. I laced up my running shoes; a nice long run would clear my head.

Mom and Robert had set up a large gym downstairs in the basement with a treadmill, elliptical, bicycle and lots of resistance and free weights. I jumped on the treadmill and started running. After a good solid hour, I felt refreshed and rejuvenated. I had a long, hot shower. When I re-entered the kitchen, Mom was putting some spaghetti into a pot over the stove.

I walked over to the fridge and pulled out a bottle of water. "Hey, Mom."

"Hi, sweetie," she said, stirring the noodles. "How was your day?"

I took a sip of my water.

"Good." I bit my lip before asking my next question. "Hey, Mom, there's a bonfire down by the lake tonight and I was wondering if I could go?"

Mom turned around to face me. She sucked her lips inward and looked like she meant business. "Who are you going with?"

"Callie. She lives next door. She was going to come over after dinner, if you want to meet her. I don't have to go if you don't want me to. It's just this thing the seniors do every year so I thought I-"

Mom laughed. "You can go. Just be home by one?"

"Thanks, Mom." I kissed her on the cheek.

"Don't mention it. I'm glad you're making friends. Want to brown the hamburger for me?"

"Sure." I walked over to the stove and picked up a spatula.

Later that night, Callie rang our doorbell at 6 o'clock sharp. I was unloading the dishwasher in the kitchen and could already hear her yapping away to Mom in the foyer. This girl seriously talked more than anyone I had ever met.

I left the dishes and met the two of them in the foyer, where it seemed like they had already become instant friends. Callie was telling Mom about her plans for college next fall, a conversation that I immensely wanted to avoid. I had no idea what my college plans were for the following year and was positive Mom would start nagging me as soon as she got the chance.

"Hi Aria!" Callie beamed at me as I walked into the room.

"Hey Cal. Come on, let's go upstairs. I'll show you my room." I grabbed her arm and steered her up the stairs.

"Nice meeting you!" Callie called back to Mom. "Your mom is really nice," she said as we entered my bedroom.

"Yeah," I sat down on my bed, "she's alright."

"She's really young," Callie commented.

"She and my dad were high school sweethearts," I explained. "They got married when they were 18, had my older sister Quinn a year later and seven years after that I was born."

"That's so romantic!" Callie gushed.

"I guess." I wrinkled my nose. "So what's the dress code for this thing anyways?"

Callie sat on my bed and glanced down at her own attire: skinny jeans, a t-shirt and a cardigan. "Casual."

"Works for me."

We spent the next hour rummaging through my clothes and gossiping. Callie gave me an overview of the people she hung out with, as well as the history of Matt Lawson. There was still a part of me that felt uneasy about him. I had never met someone so charismatic, outgoing and sure of himself. It gave me the vibe that he was into playing the field, even though Callie told me numerous times that wasn't true. I still had never had such intense chemistry with a complete stranger before; it was almost overwhelming.

It was finally time to head to the lake for the bonfire. When Callie and I got there, we were immediately bombarded by a bunch of girls from the team. I looked around for some more familiar faces and found none, no surprise. I guess I hadn't exactly been a social butterfly this week.

There were at least 50 kids at the lake; I saw a bunch of guys starting up a huge fire down by the shore. I wandered down to the water.

When I got to the shoreline, I saw Matt. He jogged over to me. "Hey, Aria! You came." I smiled. "Can I grab you a drink?" he offered.

"Just a Coke's fine," I said. I noticed some of the guys around me had beer. My mother would shoot me if she ever caught me drinking and then spend the next two hours lecturing me on teenage alcoholism and rebellion.

"Coke for me too," Matt pulled a can from the cooler opened it and passed it to me. "I don't drink," he assured me. Of course he didn't.

A guy from the fire pit called Matt. "Hey, Lawson! Stop slacking and come help me start this thing!"

"I'll be right back, Aria. Don't go anywhere."

I sipped my Coke, kicked off my flip flops and dipped one of my toes into the water. It was warm for September. Some kids were even brave enough to swim and jump off the end of the dock. I rolled up my jeans and wadded into the lake a bit.

"Aria!" a voice called out from behind me. I spun around and saw a guy I'd met walking towards me. Cody? Cory? Connor?

"Hey." I walked back to the sand.

"Connor," he extended his hand to me. I shook it. "Having fun?"

"Yeah. This is pretty cool."

Connor smiled. "It is. So hey, you're into Lawson, right?" Way to beat around the bush.

I gave Connor a half smile. "I don't really know him that well, but he seems like an alright guy." Actually, he seemed like an amazing guy; no need to let a complete stranger know that.

"He's a great guy," Connor told me. "Look, Matt is one of my best friends, and I don't really know you that well so –"

"You don't want him to get hurt," I finished for him. Well, wasn't that cute.

"Pretty much."

"Me neither," I responded.

"Good."

Just then Callie's voice called over to us from the fire. "Looks like we are wanted," I said to Connor, smiling.

"Probably more you than me," he observed dryly.

I laughed; looked like my prediction was correct. "She'll come around. Come on, let's go."

We walked over to the fire; I sat down on a log. It was just starting to get dark outside and the glow of the fire was nice and warm.

"Can I get you another drink?" I looked up and saw Matt standing in front of me.

"I'm okay. Thanks, though."

He nodded and sat down next to me. "I'm glad you came tonight, Aria. I've been looking forward to getting to know you better."

"Me too." I swallowed hard and found myself struggling for words. A stray strand of my hair was hanging in front of my eyes. Matt reached up and brushed it away, tucking it behind my ear.

"I make you nervous, don't I?" He gave me a coy smile.

I shook my head. "Nope." Then I slowly counted to 10 and focused on my breathing. If he touched me again, I may pass out.

"Just checking." He raised his eyebrows and gave a taunting smile.

We sat around the fire for a while chatting and I started to make some new friends. I slowly began to feel more comfortable about Matt and everyone else, more like my old self at least. After a while, I went down to the lake with Callie and a few girls. One of them offered me a cigarette. I refused.

"You don't smoke?" Callie asked me.

I shook my head. "You?"

"I've tried it," she admitted. "Mom and Dad would have my head if I did."

"Mine too," I laughed. We hung around by the lake for a few more minutes. Matt, Connor and a bunch of the guys came down to see what we were doing. I watched Connor and Matt whispering a few yards away from me and Callie. Matt looked over at me and back at Connor, then at Callie. A knot formed in my stomach.

"Hey Callie, I think we'd better -"

It was too late. Before I could finish my sentence, the guys were sprinting over to us. I found myself scooped up in Matt's arms as he ran down the dock.

"Don't!" I squealed. Behind me I heard Callie yelling at Connor to put her down. Before I could even blink I felt myself flying through the air and then submerged into the lake.

I pushed my legs up and kicked up to the surface. As my head came above the water, I heard Callie yell, "You guys are dead!" Matt and Connor were standing on the dock laughing.

I nodded in response, coughed up some water and started swimming towards the dock.

"It's freezing!" Callie exclaimed, swimming along beside me.

"Jerks," I muttered, shivering in the icy water. I got to the dock and Matt held out his hand to help me up. Not the smartest move. I pulled him in the lake so fast I don't even think he had time to blink.

"Hey!" He yelped as he came up for air. "That wasn't very nice."

"Oh yeah?" I said, swimming over to him. "You want to see nice?" I jumped up and dunked him under the water before he could respond.

"Well aren't you guys the cutest things," Connor called from the dock. We turned to look at him, who was nice and dry on the dock. Amy and Lauren looked at Connor with mischievous grins as they helped Callie out of the water. I watched Lauren sneak up behind him and shove him into the lake.

"Not fair!" Connor yelled coming up out of the water. I just laughed at him.

"You definitely had that one coming buddy," Matt said. I swam back to the girls and pulled myself out of the water. Matt and Connor were still goofing off in the water.

I glanced down at my now soaking wet jeans and shirt. "I'm going back to the fire!" I called.

"Me too," Callie said. "Thanks for the swim, you asses!" We walked back up the dock to the fire. Once there, I pulled off my t-shirt and left my tank top on, trying to dry myself quickly. One of Matt's friends, Scott, came over to me and Callie and handed us a towel. We graciously thanked him and attempted to air-dry ourselves.

The boys came back a few minutes later. Of course, they had both brought a change of clothes while Callie and I had not foreseen the circumstances. Matt handed me a blue hoodie.

"Here," he said. "Put this on. It'll keep you warm while your clothes dry."

"Thanks." I shrugged into his hoodie that fell down to my knees like a dress. We sat down together.

"So, you had a nice swim?" Matt teased.

"It was refreshing."

He grinned.

I looked at him. "Has anyone ever told you that you have a heartbreaking smile?" I asked.

"Only my mom every day," he said, smiling again. "She always says she's my number-one fan."

I laughed.

We stayed by the fire talking and laughing for what felt like hours. Eventually, I noticed that the sun was starting to come up. We had stayed up all night long. I looked around and saw that only Callie, Connor, Scott, Connor, Lauren, Amy, Matt and I remained at the fire.

"Hey," Connor called over to us from across the fire. "It's almost five. We were thinking of heading over to Jay's for breakfast. You guys down?"

"Do you want to go?" Matt asked me.

I checked my cell phone and didn't see any missed calls or messages from Mom. I was both surprised and concerned she hadn't called me yet. I quickly pushed those thoughts out of my mind. If you're going to stay out all night, might as well do it the right way. "I'd like that," I said.

Lauren, Callie, Matt and I got into Matt's truck and drove to Jay's. I was immediately hit with the smell of coffee when we entered the restaurant, which made me realize my stomach was growling. I was starving.

A pudgy tall man greeted us. "It's the bonfire crew," he said. "I was wondering if you were ever going to come home, princess." Callie introduced me to her dad, Mr. Jeakins.

"So you're the famous Aria."

I smiled at him. "Nice to meet you, Mr. Jeakins." The others arrived just then and the eight of us sat in a large booth at the back of the restaurant. I sipped my coffee and ordered a huge stack of pancakes, bacon and eggs.

"I like a girl that can eat," Matt commented as I shoveled food into my mouth. The pancakes were light and fluffy, the perfect texture, with a small hint of a spice that tasted like nutmeg.

I gave him a sheepish smile. "I'm so hungry and these are the best pancakes I've ever had."

"Dad's special recipe," Callie told me. "He prides himself on his pancakes."

"They are amazing," I agreed.

After devouring my breakfast I felt so full that I didn't want to leave. It was nearing 5:30, though, and I knew I was going to be dead meat when I got home. I tugged Matt's sleeve.

"I have to go," I told him. "I'm pretty sure my mom is going to kill me."

Matt nodded. "I'll drive you home."

The ride home was quick and filled with Matt singing along off-key to country love songs on the radio and me, of course, making fun of him for being a lousy singer. He didn't seem to care that he couldn't carry a tune; his confidence was refreshing and attractive. He pulled into the driveway and turned off the engine to his truck.

"I'll walk you to the door," he said

"It's okay, you don't have to -"

But he was already out of the truck and pulling my door open. I hopped out and Matt slid his hand into mine.

"Do you think you'll get in trouble?" he asked as we walked up the front steps.

"It depends on how Mom is feeling," I smirked at him. "She'll probably consider this as some form of rebellion due to us moving here. I'm sure I'll get at least a 30 minute counselling session on my 'true feelings.' It's a good thing my step-dad isn't home. That would make it a double."

Matt smiled, his classic tooth shimmering grin at me. "Well I hope it was worth it."

"It was." I looked up into his eyes. Before I knew what was happening, he leaned down and brushed his lips against mine. The kiss was soft, sweet. I felt like I was five years old again and had just woken up on Christmas morning to realize that Santa had come to bring me presents.

"Wow," Matt said, reading my mind. I just smiled, not sure how to respond. He wrapped his arms around me in an embrace that felt strong and safe. "I'll call you later?"

"Looking forward to it." I turned around, a huge grin plastered on my face, and walked towards the front door. I opened it as quietly as I possibly could and tip-toed past the living room into the kitchen. To my surprise, it was Quinn waiting for me at the kitchen table, not Mom.

"Hey, Quinnie," I said casually, using my childhood nickname for her. "How's it going?" I felt like a giddy school girl, practically prancing around her.

Quinn looked up from the huge text book her face was buried in and eye-balled me. "Did you just get home?"

"Is Mom asleep?"

"I haven't seen her and I've been home for an hour. I was working the night shift."

I sat down at the table beside her. "So, where the heck were you until six in the morning?" she asked.

"There was this grad bonfire last night. Mom said I could go."

"Mom said you could stay out all night?" Quinn raised her eyebrows. "Sure doesn't sound like the woman I grew up with."

"Well she didn't exactly say that," I made a face, puffing my cheeks out. "I lost track of time."

"You seem to be doing that a lot lately."

"So?" I said – barked, almost, though unintentionally.

"Relax," Quinn said. "I won't tell Mom you stayed out all night if that's what you're worried about."

"Really?" I flashed a grateful smile. "Thanks Quinnie, you're the best."

"I know," Quinn laughed and lightly shoved my arm. "Were you out with that guy? Matt?"

"There were other people there. A bunch of us were just talking around the fire and then some people fell asleep. We all went out for breakfast after. It was fun."

"Good," she told me. "So you really like this guy, hey?"

"He's okay." I tried to stay calm, but already felt the blush creeping up my cheeks.

"Just okay?" she teased.

"I guess." I could feel my face going even redder. "He's just really different. I don't know how to explain it."

Quinn smiled at me. "So when do we get to meet him?"

A terrified expression formed on my face. "Ha! Never if I can help it!"

Never in my life had I introduced a boy to my mother, and I definitely was not planning on doing it anytime soon. I could just see her sitting on the couch across from him, interrogating him with one hundred questions about his past and present.

"Good luck with that," Quinn shook her head at me. "I'm sure Mom will want to have him over for dinner soon."

"We aren't even going out!" I protested, throwing my hands up in the air.

"Yet," Quinn said. "Staying out all night with a guy, pretty sure you'll be dating before noon."

"Whatever!" I rolled my eyes. "I'm going to go sleep for a few hours."

"Me too," she said. "Jeremy and I are going into town this afternoon. Do you want to come? We'll probably hit up the mall."

"Maybe. I'll see what time I wake up."

"Okay. Sweet dreams, babe."

I gave her a head nod and bolted out of the kitchen and upstairs to my bedroom.

When I got to my room I put on a pair of oversized pajama pants and kept on the sweatshirt Matt had given me. I drew my blinds and collapsed on my bed, hugging the sweatshirt to my body. It smelled clean and refreshing, like springtime. I smiled, thinking about the amazing time I had. Soon enough fell into a deep sleep.

4.

I woke up a few hours later, still feeling exhausted. My joints were as stiff as a board and I was having trouble keeping my eyes open for very long. I slowly dragged myself out of bed and headed downstairs to the kitchen with visions of a steaming mug of coffee in my mind.

Mom and Quinn were sitting at the table together, coffee cups in hand.

"Morning," I muttered, making my way to the cupboard.

"Good morning, Aria!" Mom greeted me in her normal, too-cheerful morning voice.

I grabbed a mug from the top shelf, poured myself some coffee and chugged half of it down in one gulp. I poured some more and sat down with them at the table.

"Late night?" Quinn commented. I shot her a look.

"How was the bonfire?" Mom asked. "Did you have fun?"

"Yeah," I said, taking a sip of my coffee. "It was lots of fun."

"Did you meet some new friends?"

"Yeah. A few."

"Excellent!" Mom exclaimed. "I'm glad you're starting to like it here."

Like it? Who said anything about liking it here? I just nodded at her and continued sipping my coffee.

"Did you get in late?" she asked.

I glanced down at the floor. "Not too late."

"Well, that's good," she said. I was surprised she wasn't commenting on my body language and bursting out with accusations of staying out past curfew.

The phone rang and Quinn picked it up.

"Aria, it's for you," she said, passing me the phone.

"Who is it?" A pained expression formed on my face.

"Callie," she said. I took the phone from her hand.

"Hello?" I said.

"Aria!" Callie's familiar, loud voice shouted clearly from the other end of the line. "Get dressed. We're going down to the basketball courts to get some practice in. I'll be over in 15 minutes."

"I don't know -" I started to say, then realizing that it was too late. She had already hung up the phone. "I'm going to play basketball with Callie and some of the girls," I said to Mom.

"Will you be home for dinner?" she asked.

"Should be." The phone rang in my hand again, startling me. "Hello?"

"Aria?"

"Yes..."

"Hey, it's Matt." His voice was soft in my ear. My eyes widened and I swear my heart skipped a beat.

"Oh. Hey." I shot a glance at Mom and Quinn who were both looking at me.

"I just wanted to see what you were doing tonight? Did you maybe want to meet up later?"

"I'm going to play basketball with some of the girls now," I told him. "But later on tonight sounds good."

"Nice," he said. "I was thinking I could take you out for dinner?"

"Dinner? Sure, dinner would be great."

"Awesome. I'll pick you up at six then?"

I hesitated. "I can meet you there."

"No, no. I'll pick you up."

"Okay then. I'll see you tonight."

"Bye, Aria." I hung up the phone. I took a deep breath and waited for what I knew was coming next.

"Who was that?" Quinn's words practically jumped at me.

"Just a friend."

"A boy friend?" Mom asked.

"Yeah," I sighed. Mom and Quinn exchanged smiles across the table. "So I guess I won't be home for dinner tonight after all."

"That's fine," Mom replied. "Robert gets in tonight anyways."

Super.

"I wish you didn't roll your eyes like that every time I say his name," she said. Busted.

"Sorry," I said mechanically, even though I wasn't sorry. I shifted uncomfortably.

"Don't you have to go play basketball?" Quinn asked. I smiled at her, grateful for an interruption.

"Sure do. See you guys later!" I jetted out of the kitchen.

I jogged over to the basketball courts to meet Callie and the girls for a brutal practice. All afternoon Callie had us running wind sprints, doing conditioning drills, lay ups, free throws, you name it. This girl put a new meaning into "intense." I felt like my date with Matt would never come. When she finally let us go, I felt like I had an extra 50 pounds strapped to my legs all the way home.

I got ready carefully and tried to disregard the tightness that was beginning to form in my chest. I find dinner dates slightly terrifying. I hadn't been on many, and always thought them to be awkward. Even though I knew Matt and I had already hung out several times and it had been fine, my hands were clammy and I still found myself worrying.

I went downstairs where Mom and Robert had just returned home from the airport. It had been nice having Robert out of the house and I wished he could have just stayed away. When he was around, I always felt like he was inspecting me. We exchanged small talk for a few minutes, while I nervously stole glances at the clock.

"Where are you off to tonight?" Robert asked me.

"Just going to dinner with a friend."

"Anyone I know?"

"His name is Matt."

"Does he have a last name?" Robert smiled at me. I held back my eye roll. Talk about the third degree. It was bad enough having a mother with a Ph.D in feelings who wanted to analyze every move I made, but now I was getting the same deal from my hot-shot psychologist step-father.

"Lawson."

"Ah." Robert looked as though he was having some sort of eureka moment. "Peter Lawson's boy?"

"Sure?" I raised my eyebrows. "I'm not sure who his parents are. His dad is a principal."

"That's Peter alright," Robert smiled again. Was I missing something? "Peter and I went to high school together," Robert explained. "I've met Matt a few times. He's a good kid."

"Glad you approve," I said sarcastically.

"Aria…" Mom's warning tone. She averted her eyes from reading the newspaper and gave Robert a head nod of approval. "Be home by midnight?" Even though she asked it like a question, I knew it wasn't.

"Yeah. Sure." I watched as the digital clock on the oven changed from 5:59 to 6:00. Just like clockwork, the doorbell rang. "See ya!" I started to run out of the kitchen but Robert was already a few steps ahead of me. He walked to the front door with me shuffling nervously behind him and Mom prancing after me.

Matt looked incredible. He was wearing jeans and a blue button-down shirt that made the blue in his eyes pop. He was shrugged into a sharp jet-black blazer. His blond hair was neatly combed, only a small strand fell in his eyes like glistening rays of sunshine. I let out my breath in a whoosh.

Mom lightly put a hand on my shoulder as Robert introduced her. They made small talk for a few minutes. Robert asked Matt how his parents were doing.

"Have her home by midnight," Robert spoke in an authoritative voice. My shoulders tensed. It took every ounce of willpower not to roll my eyes at him. I didn't like it when he tried to act all father-figure around me.

Mom must have sensed this. She squeezed my shoulders gently. "Have fun tonight, sweetheart." She smiled at Matt. "It was nice meeting you, Matt."

"Nice meeting you Mrs. Br – err- McDermott," Matt stumbled over the words but caught himself quickly and then flashed Mom his trademark grin. I pulled him out onto the porch and closed the door behind us. "That wasn't so bad," Matt said with confidence. "I think your mom likes me."

"I think the fact you weren't dressed like a drug dealer and came sober wins you brownie points."

Matt widened his eyes. "And what exactly does a drug dealer dress like?"

I laughed. "Couldn't tell you, but you definitely got the Mom look of approval."

"Glad I passed the test."

"Me too."

We drove into the city for dinner and went to a small Greek restaurant on the coastline. We sat at a small table that overlooked the ocean. The restaurant was dimly lit and intimate. An older man was strumming a guitar on a small stage. The calm music gave the restaurant a peaceful feel.

"This place is really nice," I commented.

"Glad you like it." He grabbed my hand across the table and interlaced his fingers through mine. His hand was soft and warm.

The food was amazing and the portions were massive. Matt ordered us the restaurant's special linguine with a red tomato clam sauce. The tomato sauce had the perfect amount of juiciness with just the right touch of spices that were explosive on my taste buds. Matt polished off his plate but we had to get mine in a to-go box. We left the restaurant with extremely full stomachs. Half of me was ready to find a couch somewhere and have a cat nap, but Matt told me he had a surprise for me.

"What kind of surprise?" I asked curiously.

"You'll see." Matt gave me a mysterious sort of smile. We stopped at a coffee place and got two cups of coffee to go. Matt said we had to drive a little further.

When we stopped, it took me a minute to realize where we were. The beach. The first day Matt and I had met I had told him how much I loved the ocean. I obviously didn't get to see it much living in Toronto my whole life; I had to settle for lakes.

Matt got out of the car and walked around to the passenger side to open my door for me.

"I can't believe we are at the beach." I stared at him completely awestruck.

"I remembered you saying it was one of your favourite places," Matt said. He grabbed my hand. "Let's walk." I felt like my heart was pounding through my chest.

"You're pretty amazing, you know that?"

Matt grinned. "Well, I am a pretty big deal."

"And oh so humble!" I rolled my eyes.

"You like it." He leaned down and kissed me lightly on the lips. I felt like I was floating on air.

We stayed at the beach for an hour or so. He brought a blanket for us to sit on. Nothing felt more right than lying under the stars with Matt's arms around me. When he announced it was time to go home, I was disappointed.

"Can't have you missing curfew on your first night out with me," he said firmly. "I don't want Rob to give me a hard time." I felt a slight twinge of annoyance at the mention of Robert's name but reluctantly agreed.

After the hour-long car ride home, Matt walked me to my porch. "So there's something I've been meaning to ask you…" I shifted nervously wondering what it could be.

"I don't usually do this on my first real date with someone, but it feels different this time." I could feel my heart pounding like it was going to beat right out of my chest. "Aria," he said, "will you be my girlfriend?"

"Yes!" I squealed loudly. My words pounced at him like a tiger ready for feeding. "Of course I'll be your girlfriend." He ducked his head down towards mine and kissed me. That one kiss said all the words in the world. It was magical.

The date was perfect. In fact if there was a better word to describe perfect that would have summed up our date. Matt was a gentleman. I had never been out with anyone like him before. He treated me like I was a Princess and looked at me like I was the only girl in the room.

That night I laid in bed wide awake. My mind was crawling with thoughts of Matt. It was strange to me that I had only known him for a week. Part of me felt like I had known him my whole life. All the fears I had about him, all the worries just seemed to melt away every time I saw his smiling face.

5.

On Monday at school everyone knew that Matt and I were an item. I was assuming Callie was the one who had pushed this through the gossip mill. She seemed even more excited than me and instantly started babbling about how great Matt was and how great I was, and how she was so ecstatic we were together. People I didn't even know were coming up to me and commenting on my new relationship. This definitely was doing wonders for my popularity at a new school.

Matt met me at my locker between classes, held my hand as he walked me down the hall and left me with a kiss at the door of every classroom. He was very chivalrous and it was refreshing. None of the guys I had dated back home were anything like him.

After school, Callie met me at my locker. We had basketball tryouts. "You ready?" she asked me.

"Of course," I told her, praying that I looked as confident as I was trying to sound.

Back at home, basketball had been easy and natural for me. I had always been the best player on the team, always was the team captain and never had anyone around to threaten my status. Here, I wasn't sure where I stood. A lot of the girls on the team looked like they were pretty good.

"You are going to do awesome," Callie told me. It was like she was reading my thoughts or something.

"Thanks."

Try-outs were pretty typical. We started with conditioning, something I had never had an issue with. Push-ups, wind sprints, laps, cross overs. By the end of this, 12 of us still standing. Two girls were in the bathroom puking; three more had already given up and hit the sidelines.

"Freshmen," Callie nodded towards them. "They think they are big enough deals to make varsity. Coach and I think it's fun to torture them." I laughed.

Coach Matthews was your typical basketball coach. She was to-the-point, intense and didn't put up with crap. I had her for fitness as well and thought she was a good teacher so far. She blew her whistle.

"Okay ladies! Scrimmage time. Callie, you captain one team. Aria, you take the other."

"Really?" I was surprised.

"I told you," Callie said. "You know your stuff. Clearly Coach thinks so too."

The scrimmage was fun and natural. It felt so nice to play again. I bounced the basketball and felt the soft leather against my fingertips. I shot a three-pointer and sunk it.

"Way to go, Aria!" Matt's voice hollered from across the gymnasium. I looked up to see Matt and a few guys standing by the bleachers watching us. I grinned.

"Nice fan club!" Callie called from across the court. I felt my cheeks burning a dark shade of red.

"Looks like you could use one," I shot back. I called out for the ball, lazily ran under the hoop for a layup and scored.

"Show off," Callie laughed.

A few minutes later, Coach Matthews called us in to recap the end of day one. She told us the final tryouts would be tomorrow. I had no doubt in my mind about making the team. I knew I had rocked it. Callie and I walked over to where the boys were standing.

"Nice game ladies," Matt flashed us both a grin.

"Thanks," I beamed at him.

"A few of us are going to get some pizza," Matt said. "You girls interested?"

"Sounds good," Callie replied.

I hesitated. "I can for a bit, but I have a lot of homework."

"Homework?" Matt made a face. "You mean you actually do that?" It took me a second to realize he was kidding.

"Only on my good days."

"Let's hit the showers," Callie grabbed my arm. "Wait here." She instructed Matt, who nodded at her in response.

A long hot shower was just what I needed after tryouts. I let the hot water pound down on my shoulders and inhaled deeply.

"So here's a question for you," I peered at Callie over the wall separating our showers. "How do you get any studying done hanging out with those guys?"

Callie raised her eyebrows, "Ah, you mean the 'let's go for pizza,' 'let's have a bon fire,' 'let's go to every place in the world but the library' crew?"

I laughed. "I guess so. I'm just up to my ears in homework already and don't know how I'm supposed to get any of it done!"

"I don't sleep much," Callie admitted. "I've never been too fond of it anyways. And I've always done pretty well in school."

"One of those I-don't-need-to-study-and-can-still-get-an-A types?" I asked.

She gave me a small smile. "Something like that, I suppose."

"You suck." I stuck my tongue out at her and turned back to my shower.

Pizza was fun. We rounded up Amy and Lauren from the team and went to Pizza Pizza, an arcade-like pizza joint in town. They had video games, pool tables and big over-sized booths that felt like you were sitting on a castle throne.

Matt slung his arm loosely over my shoulder in the booth. Callie sat on the other side of me; across from us sat Lauren and Amy. Scott and Connor were playing pool over in the corner. I noticed Callie's eyes wander over to Connor for a moment and then look directly back down to the table top in front of her.

"Connor's pretty cute," I whispered in her ear. She shrugged in response and took a sip of her Diet Coke. I elbowed her as Connor and Scott came to our table. "He's coming over here."

"Any of you up for some doubles?" Scott asked.

"I'm good man," Matt squeezed my shoulder.

"Callie?" Conner spoke this time but Callie was in another world. I followed her gaze and saw that Logan and a group of guys had just walked in the front door and sat down at a booth. I coughed loudly, breaking through her trance.

Callie snapped back to life. "I should probably get going guys. I have a lot of chemistry homework tonight."

"I'll drive you home," Matt offered, also staring at Logan. He jumped up from his seat and tossed some bills on the table. "Here you go, ladies. See you guys later!" He grabbed my hand and I quickly grabbed onto Callie as Matt steered us out of the restaurant.

"Where's the fire?" I asked as we stepped outside. The air was getting chilly now and I shivered in the night.

"Sorry," he said. He opened the door for me and I climbed into the truck; he did the same for Callie who climbed into the back, then he closed the door and ran around to sit in the driver's seat.

Matt started the engine to the truck and then turned around to face Callie. "Are you okay?" he asked her. He looked concerned. She nodded.

"I just want to go home," Callie said, her voice as small as a mouse's. I felt like I was missing something.

Matt dropped Callie off first and got out of the truck with her.

"Be right back," he told me. Callie and I exchanged goodbyes. I watched as Matt and Callie chatted outside his truck. She looked upset. He walked her to the door, gave her a hug and ran back to the truck.

"Sorry about that," he gave me a small smile as he started up the truck again.

"Everything okay?" I asked.

"Callie and Logan had a really bad break-up," he said without elaborating.

"She mentioned it."

"She's still having a rough time," Matt said, pulling the truck into my driveway.

I smiled at him. "Well I'm glad she has you as a friend."

He smiled back and leaned over to lightly kiss me on the cheek. "You are amazing," he told me.

"Why thank you," I smiled at him. "Call me later."

"You can count on it."

I got out of the car and skipped all the way to the front door. I let myself in and went into the kitchen where I heard movement.

"Mom?" I called. "Quinn?"

"It's me." I heard Robert's cheerful voice call. I sighed as I walked through the kitchen door. "How was your day?" he asked.

56

"It was fine."

"Are you enjoying your new school so far?"

"It's alright."

"You're getting home pretty late," he commented.

"It's only 6."

"I meant for school getting out." He moved over to the stove to stir something.

"Oh." I bit my lip. A nervous habit I had. "I had basketball tryouts."

"That's great!" Robert exclaimed with excitement. A little too much excitement, if you ask me.

"I guess so."

"Do you think you are going to make the team?"

"Yeah."

He sighed and gave me a look that said he was feeling uncomfortable. Then he decided to push past it and go straight for the gold. "So how are things with Matt? You two seem close."

I pursed my lips. "Fine. Is my mom home?"

Another sigh. "Yes. She's in her office."

"Thanks." I started to walk out of the kitchen.

"Dinner will be ready in 10 minutes!" he called after me.

"I already ate!" I hollered back and ran up the stairs to my bedroom.

I attempted to spend the next hour buried in my chemistry notes, but my mind had other plans for me. I had never been so distracted in my life. One half of me was completely ecstatic, glowing like she was walking on sunshine; the other half felt irritated and trapped in this new place with new rules, plus a new parent.

My phone rang on my desk in front of me. "Hello?"

"Aria. Hey."

Matt.

"Hi," I said, smiling. "How's it going?"

"Not bad," he said. "Just bored. Wondering if you wanted to go for a walk?"

"A walk?" I echoed. "Sure?"

"Cool. So, I don't live that far from you. I was thinking we could meet halfway? Just walk down Cherry like you are heading to the lake? My house is to the right on Brown."

"Sounds good. See you soon." I pulled on a sweater and a warm jacket and went downstairs.

Mom and Robert were in the living room watching TV. I walked in to tell Mom where I was going, but before I could even get out the words Robert beat me to it.

"Going out?" he asked.

I fixed my eyes on Mom. "I was just going to go for a walk with Matt."

"It's a school night," Robert commented. I took a deep breath. If he would have been standing in front of me, I would have been more tempted to kick him or punch him in the face.

"Please Mom? Just for an hour?" I gave her a pleading look. Mom had never been big on rules. Of course, she was a psychologist and insisted that we tell her everything and communicate all things to her, but she was pretty cool with letting us go places.

Mom looked at me and then at Robert, a torn expression on her face. "Just for an hour?" She looked at Robert for confirmation. He grunted and then nodded slowly.

"Thanks!" I smiled. "You're the greatest. See you in a bit."

Jordan Falls was beautiful in autumn. The streets were lit up with brown, red and orange leaves. Everywhere you looked were big beautiful trees that appeared old but full of life. I walked down my street and could hear the crunch of the leaves under my shoes. I loved that sound and the fresh, distinct smell of fall. To me, it always smelled like someone was having a campfire down the road. This was probably the only thing I didn't miss about the city, getting to see the true seasons exploding in nature.

After a few minutes of walking, I saw Matt coming towards me.

"Hey," he called.

"Hey yourself," I called back. We came face to face and he gave me a quick hug. "So, where are we walking?"

"I was thinking we could go to the park," Matt suggested.

"Lead the way, captain."

We walked a few minutes away to an elementary school where Matt told me his Dad worked.

"I'll show you something cool." He led me over to a huge colourful mural on the side of the building. He pointed to a handprint on the wall. It was a small green handprint, one of a little boy. "That's my hand! From grade two. This was our unity mural."

"It's so little," I commented. "Cute. Hey! Monkey bars!" I ran over to the monkey bars and started to swing myself across them. This was a favourite childhood activity of mine. Somehow, it seemed a lot harder now. My hands began to slip and I slid off the bars, landing on the ground. "Hey, this is hard!" I yelled.

Matt just laughed. "Good effort."

"Let's see you do better." I watched as Matt walked over to the monkey bars, jumped up on them, and lazily pulled his body across them. "Show off!" He just shook his head at me.

Time always flew by when I was with Matt. I felt like the time we spent together was never enough. We ended our night on the swings together where he gave me a gentle goodnight kiss.

"I'm really glad I met you, Aria Brooks." He flashed me that grin again.

"I'm really glad I met you too, Matthew Lawson." And then I ran all the way home so that I wouldn't miss my one-hour deadline with Mom.

I let myself in to a dark house and went straight to my room, hoping I could get some studying done before bed. I had just started on my first practice problem when I heard a tap on my door.

"Aria?" Mom called. "Can I come in?"

I sighed and closed my chemistry textbook. So much for that. "Sure."

She opened the door. "How was your night with Matt?"

I couldn't help it, I smiled. "It was good."

"We didn't really get to talk much this weekend." Mom pushed a strand of her blonde hair behind her ear and sat on my bed. She smiled at me.

My mom had sat me down the day I turned 13 and talked to me about sex and becoming a woman. Back home, the boys I dated never even made it through the front door. Needless to say, seeing me smiling about a boy was new to her.

"You guys seem to be spending a lot of time together so far."

"Yeah," I said, and then something inside me shifted. I decided to give her a bit of a break. "He asked me out the other night."

"Really?" She smiled at me. "Well, I think that's great! I'm glad you are making new friends. I just want you to be happy."

"Thanks, Mom."

She stood up and kissed me on the forehead. "You're welcome, sweetheart. I love you."

"I love you too." I said, smiling back. She stood in the doorway, hovering like there was something she wanted to say. I took a deep breath. "Everything okay, Mom?"

"What?" She bit her lower lip; this was very uncharacteristic of her.

"You looked like you were going to say something."

"Oh. Really?" Her blue eyes met mine. "No. I'm sorry. I supposed I just dozed for a second. I was just thinking..." She let her voice trail off.

"Mom! You are freaking me out!"

"I was just thinking about your father." She gave me a small smile. "You never brought a boy home before. I was just imagining how he would have dealt with it all."

"I think Dad would have liked Matt," I offered.

"Oh, me too," she affirmed. "I just miss him, that's all."

"Me too." Tears sprung to my eyes quickly. I shook my head as if to quickly shake them away. "Mom?"

"Yes?"

"Thanks." I stood up, crossed the padded carpet and hugged her.

"For what?" She took a step back.

I hesitated. "For what you just said. It's nice to know that you miss him too." She stared at me for a moment, a puzzled expression on her face.

"Oh Aria." She sighed and cupped my face in her hands, looking at me with the saddest eyes I had ever seen. "I should let you get back to work." She motioned towards my textbooks.

"Yes. Good idea." I pretended not to notice the new scent of awkwardness that floated in the air between us. I flopped down on my bed and cracked open my chemistry book. It looked like I had a long night ahead of me.

6.

Sunlight streamed through the window into the corners of my closed eyelids. I slowly opened my eyes and arched my neck backwards. I looked at my alarm clock and saw it was 8:02 a.m. Crap! I must have fallen asleep studying last night and was now going to be late for school.

I jumped out of bed and threw on the first clothes I saw, scooped up my textbooks and ran downstairs and directly into Quinn who was walking out of the kitchen.

"Where's the fire?" she asked.

"I have 15 minutes to get to chemistry," I explained. I draped a jacket over my shoulders and quickly put on my shoes. Quinn was still in her hospital scrubs.

"I'll drive you," she told me. "Let's go."

"Have I told you that you are the best sister in the world?"

"Yeah, yeah," she said. "Just add this to the tab."

Thanks to Quinn, I made it to school in record time. I sprinted past an ever-so-chivalrous Matt who was waiting at my locker, planted a kiss on his cheek and continued down the hallway to class.

The chemistry quiz was a nightmare. About halfway through, I realized I had no idea what a catalyst was and knew I should have read the chapter before coming to class. We marked the quizzes in class and I was not surprised to see the big fat "F" marked at the top of mine. I smacked my head on the desk. This was going to be a long day.

And long it was. In history, we were assigned a research project on the aftermath of World War II in Canada. Luckily, it was partner-paired; Matt claimed me as his partner. In English we had a pop quiz. My knowledge of literature saved me there.

Next was fitness, where we got to see the results for basketball tryouts. I saw that I made the team! Practice started tomorrow after school. Now I just needed to do about a million discussion questions, catch up on two chapters worth of chemistry reading and start a history project.

By the end of the day I was ready to curl up in bed. I definitely wasn't looking forward to the mound of homework that awaited me. Thankfully, Matt met me on the front steps at the end of the day to take me to his house, where we were going to work on our history project.

"Hey beautiful," he greeted me. He wrapped me in his arms, his tall frame towering over me. "You ready?"

"Let's go."

Matt's house was huge. It was one of those mansions you read about in books or see on TV shows, not houses you just happened upon in everyday life. It had a brick exterior, a lawn the size of a football field and a massive steel pole fence and hedges surrounding the perimeter.

"This is where you live?" I gaped as we pulled into the driveway. Matt walked around to my side of the truck to let me out.

"Home sweet home," he said.

"You didn't tell me you were part of the royal family."

"Funny."

"You live in a castle." I pointed this out because he seemed blatantly unaware.

"Your house is pretty nice too."

"Not like this," I said, staring at the humungous building in front of me, barely capable of imagining what the inside would look like.

"Can you stop gaping so we can go inside?"

"Sorry." I quickly regained my focus and Matt led me up the massive stone staircase to his front door.

He opened the front door and a swarm of sound immediately hit my ears. I heard a piano playing loudly, a television blaring, the sound of footprints banging on the floor above us and lots of voices. This was definitely nothing like my house, which sounded more like a university library.

A little girl with curly blonde hair and eyes as blue as Matt's ran up and threw her arms around his legs.

"Mattie, you're home!" she squealed. Matt kneeled down on the ground and wrapped his arms around the little girl.

"Ruthie," he said, standing back up. "This is Aria. Aria, this is my youngest sister Ruthie."

"And favouritest." Ruthie smiled at him.

"And favouritest." Matt winked at me.

"Hi Ruthie," I held out my hand to her. "Nice to meet you." She looked at my hand for a few seconds and then laughed. She wrapped me in a big hug.

"Matt says you're his girlfriend," she looked at me questioningly.

I smiled at her. "Matt's right."

"I asked Mom if I could have a boyfriend and she said no way!" Ruthie made a face and I laughed. "And Dad said I couldn't have one until I was in college like Rachel!" I laughed again.

"It's okay," I told her. "Boyfriends are kind of yucky anyways."

"Ouch!" Matt held both his hands over his heart, pretending to look wounded.

"Don't be such a baby!" I teased.

"Such a heartbreaker," Matt sighed. "Okay, let's go introduce you to the rest of the clan. Lead the way, Ruthie."

We followed Ruthie into the kitchen where we were hit with a circus of children – no joke. I looked around the room. A boy and a girl, each around 10 years old, sat at the kitchen table doing homework. A tall girl who looked around our age was helping them. A group of boys were running around playing with Nerf guns in the split-level family room below. And somewhere in the house I heard a piano being played by someone who sounded like they needed a bit of work.

The older girl looked up as we walked into the kitchen. "Hey guys." She smiled at me. "You must be Aria;

I'm Rachel, Matt's older sister." She held out her hand to me and I shook it. "Nice to meet you," she said.

"Nice to meet you too." I studied her profile. This girl was knock-out gorgeous. She looked to be about six feet tall, model thin and had straight, dark chocolate brown hair. She also had the ocean blue eyes that seemed to run in this family. Her skin looked delicate, like a porcelain doll.

"This is Adam and Anna." Rachel pointed to the boy and the girl at the table who both had similar physical traits.

"You have a lot of brothers and sisters." My eyes widened.

Matt laughed. "Aria has one sister."

"Ah," Rachel's eyes twinkled. "Well, you are in for a treat today. Hey Micah, come meet Matt's new girlfriend!" A boy who looked almost like a mini Matt ran upstairs into the kitchen. He looked to be about 13 or 14 years old.

"Hey," he nodded at me. "I'm Micah."

"I'm Aria," I said. "Nice to meet you."

"Is Dad home?" Matt asked.

"Not yet," Rachel told him. "Mom's still teaching."

"I have ears."

I frowned at Matt's comment. Rachel looked over at me. "Mom's a piano teacher," she said, motioning towards the music coming from the other room.

"Ah, that explains that off-key playing."

"Do you play?" she asked me.

"I did when I was younger," I made a disgusted face. "I hated it, though."

"Me too," she said sympathetically. "Mom was crushed that I wasn't going to be the next family musician. She's tried with all of us."

"No luck?"

"Micah plays. He prefers the guitar, though."

I looked questioningly at Matt. "You guys all have Bible names, hey?"

"That's all Dad," he told me.

"Do you go to church?" Rachel interrupted.

I paused. "Sometimes. I haven't been in a while."

"You should come with us sometime," she offered.

"Sure," I said. I felt uncomfortable. The last time I had been in a church was at Dad's funeral. When Dad was alive we had gone to church every Sunday. Ever since he died, something inside of me made me not want to even be on the same block as a church.

"Easy Rachel," Matt said. "Aria's still new here."

"I know, I know," Rachel held up both her hands. "So, how do you like Jordan Falls, Aria?"

"It's a lot smaller than I'm used to," I offered. "But I really like the people." I smiled at Matt.

"Clearly she's blind," Rachel teased and punched Matt lightly on the arm.

He smiled at me. "Clearly."

An older woman came into the kitchen and scooped up Ruthie, who was playing on the floor, into her arms. "How are my favourite children today?"

"Mom," Matt cleared his throat. "There's someone I want you to meet." His mother put Ruthie down and turned to face us.

"You must be Aria," she said, taking both of my hands into her own. "I'm Carol, Matt's mom. Matt has told me so much about you." She hugged me like we were old friends and I instantly felt comfortable around her. "It's so nice to meet you. You look just as beautiful as Matt mentioned."

"Nice to meet you too," I laughed. "And thank you." I liked this woman. She had a certain spunkiness about her, and I could definitely see where Matt got his good looks from.

"What are you guys up to this afternoon?" She walked over to the fridge and began pulling containers out of it.

"We are going to work on our history project," Matt told her.

"You can work in your father's study. He won't be home until dinner. Aria, would you like to stay for dinner?"

"Sure," I said. "I just need to call my mom and make sure it's okay with her."

"Let's go get started." Matt took me by the hand and started to pull me out of the kitchen.

"But I wanted to show Aria my dolls!" Ruthie protested.

"You can show her after," Matt said, ruffling her hair with his hand. "We have to study." He took me down another hallway and led me into a massive room that more resembled a library than a study. The walls were lined with bookshelves, and there were couches and two big desks.

I walked over to the books and began to browse the titles.

"What are you looking for?" Matt asked me, closing the door before following me across the room.

"A secret passageway."

"Very funny."

"Your house is awesome," I smiled at him.

"I'm glad you like it." He walked over to me and kissed me on the lips. The door to the study opened and Ruthie walked in.

"Mom asked me to bring you a snack," she held up a plate of cookies.

"Oh did she?" Matt asked, shaking his head.

"Yep," Ruthie smiled secretively.

"How convenient. Okay, scram squirt. We need to study." Ruthie ran out of the room. "Mom likes to check up on me," he explained.

"That's cute."

"Sure. Cute." He grabbed his history textbook. "Let's get to work, slacker."

We spent the next two hours engrossed in our project. I was surprised with how disciplined Matt was when it came to school. We finished the project and felt that it was good work, too. Then it was time for dinner. Matt led me out of the study and into the dining room, where I was introduced to his dad.

Peter Lawson reminded me a lot of my own father. He was loud, friendly and playful with his children. He had a smile on his face that could cover acres. The second he met me, he said, "So, you're the girl my son's going to marry, eh?"

I almost choked on my water. Matt turned a deep shade of purple. "Oh Pete," Carol said, shaking her head at her husband. "Don't be so dramatic. They're just kids."

"Dad's a real joker," Rachel chimed in. Everyone laughed.

Matt's family was so much different from mine now. First off, I wasn't used to having nine people at the dinner table, but there was just something different about them. They were so genuine and real and made me feel like I belonged there with them. His parents looked at each other the way that Mom and Dad used to look at each other. I have never seen Mom and Robert look at each other that way.

Dinner passed quickly, most of it spent with Matt's parents asking about myself and my family. Meeting someone's family says a lot about a person in my mind. It can border between sanity and insanity; that's what my mother says, anyways. You never want to make things serious with anyone until you see where they come from. By the end of the evening, I felt like I knew even more about Matt.

After dinner, Matt drove me home. "They loved you," he told me, kissing me on the cheek.

"I loved them," I smiled adoringly at him. "Your family is wonderful –," I paused.

"What is it?" Matt asked.

Tears filled my eyes and I quickly brushed them away. "They just remind me of the way my family used to be. When my dad was here."

Matt put his arms around me. "You must really miss him. I can't even imagine."

I took a deep breath. "I feel like part of me died when he did. Sometimes I come home and I think he's going to be there, waiting for me. Then I remember he's gone."

"I'm sorry," Matt said. "I wish you didn't have to feel that way." I didn't say anything. I didn't know if there was anything I could say. I just stood there on the front porch in Matt's arms, feeling like there was nothing in the world that could break us apart.

7.

The next few weeks passed by quickly and I began to develop a routine in Jordan Falls. I became entwined in a life of Matt, Callie, homework, school and basketball. However, most of my focus went to Matt and basketball. I had practice Monday to Thursday every day after school. Matt would wait around for me after practice, then we'd go to his house for dinner. I truly felt like I was a member of their family now and loved spending time with them. After dinner, we would do our homework together and then I would go home, sneak past Mom and Robert with as few words as possible and go to sleep.

It was Thanksgiving weekend. Ironically, I had been dreading this holiday all month. It was our first Thanksgiving without Dad and our first Thanksgiving with Robert, probably one of the reasons why I was avoiding my mother. When Dad was alive, we always celebrated Thanksgiving the same way. We cooked a huge turkey dinner, and when it was ready we sat around the table and say what we were thankful for. After dinner, we stuffed ourselves with pie and watched football on the couch until we all fell asleep. It didn't sound like much, but it was tradition. Part of me wanted to skip Thanksgiving entirely this year. Too many memories I didn't think I could handle.

The Friday before Thanksgiving weekend, we had a half-day at school. I had chemistry last period of the day; we were told we'd spend the remainder of the class going over last week's unit tests. When I got mine back, I saw I had failed, which meant I was currently failing the class. I felt like throwing up.

My teacher kindly explained that if we had gotten lower then a C minus, we needed to get our exams signed by a parent and brought back the following week. This seemed ridiculous to me. I was 17 years old; why did I need my mommy to sign my exam for me?

"I'm screwed," I said to Callie as we walked out of the classroom. "My mom is going to kill me, *then* she is going to ground me."

"I'm sure it won't be that bad," Callie said.

I moaned. "My sister is a science prodigy, and my mother is a psychologist. It's going to be bad!"

"I can tutor you," Callie offered.

"That would be awesome. If I don't get my grade up, I'm going to be pulled from the basketball team."

"We'll get your grade up," she assured me. "We have another test right before Halloween. You'll be fine."

"If you say so," I shrugged.

"Positive attitude," Callie said as we got to my locker. It was weird to see Matt wasn't there waiting for me today. He and his family had gone to spend the weekend in Victoria with his grandparents.

I got my textbooks out of my locked and slammed it shut, walking down the hallway. "I guess I better go get this over with," I said as I walked towards the door. "It was nice knowing you."

"Good luck!" she called down the hall after me.

When I got home, I saw Mom's car in the driveway. I cursed silently. I had half-hoped she would be working at the hospital today. I opened the front door and heard voices coming from the living room. Mom and Quinn were sitting on the couch talking.

"She lives!" Quinn shrieked as I walked into the room.

I frowned at her. "What's that supposed to mean?"

"Hmm. I don't know, maybe that I haven't seen you in a month."

"You're exaggerating."

"Am I?" Her eyes widened at me. "When was the last time I saw you?"

I shrugged at her. "I've been busy," I offered meekly.

"With Matt," she grinned at me.

"With life!"

"And Matt."

"You are so annoying."

Mom laughed. "It is nice to see you, sweetheart." She kissed me on the cheek. "I have a 2 o'clock appointment, so I'll be in my office. We are doing dinner tomorrow night, okay?"

"Sure," I said numbly.

"Quinn doesn't work tomorrow night and Robert's parents are coming in from the city."

"Sure," I said again. Mom left the room and I shuddered.

"What was that?" Quinn asked me.

"What?"

"Your little shudder over there." Quinn took her straight, long, blonde hair in her hands and pulled in back into a ponytail.

"I guess I'm just nervous about this weekend."

"It will be weird," Quinn agreed. "It'll be okay, though. Have you talked to her about it?"

"Who?"

"Mom."

"Why would I?"

"Because," Quinn told me, "it'll make you feel better."

"Have *you* talked to her about it?" I pointed out.

Quinn smiled at me. "Actually, I have."

"Really?" I sat down on the couch beside her.

"I talk to Mom about Dad a lot. I think it's important."

"I think it's awkward."

"He was my dad for 23 years," Quinn said. "This first run of holidays without him won't be easy for anyone. Don't pretend otherwise. Mom isn't stupid, she knows. She just feels like she needs to walk on glass around you."

"She told you that?"

"No," Quinn said. "But I know Mom. I know there's no way in the world she would have let you run around for three weeks without seeing any of us before Dad died. She's just trying to let you deal with everything."

I sank back into the couch cushions. "I'm just so mad, Quinnie."

"I know you are, babe," Quinn put her hand lightly on my shoulder. "Sooner or later, though, you are going to have to deal with it."

"So," I said abruptly changing the subject. "Want to sign my chemistry test I failed?"

Quinn laughed. "Good luck with that one, little sister." She shook her head and stood up, heading towards the kitchen.

I spent the next few hours trying to avoid Mom. This was easy, seeing as she was cooped up in her office most of the afternoon. Quinn and I were in the kitchen starting dinner. While she was doing most of the cooking, I was staring out the back window at Mom's office.

"Just go talk to her," Quinn told me. "Get it over with. I can tutor you for the rest of the semester and everything will be fine."

"She's going to be mad."

"When in your whole life have you ever seen our mother get angry?" Quinn picked up a knife and began chopping a pile of celery stalks.

I bit my lip. "You know what I mean. Her disappointed face. I can't handle it."

She grabbed me by the shoulders and led me to the backdoor. "Go!" I shrugged my feet into a pair of flats.

"I don't want to."

Quinn opened the backdoor and pushed me out. "I don't care. Go talk to her so I don't need to watch you freak out about this all weekend."

"You suck."

"I love you too." Quinn gave me a fake smile and shut the door in my face.

I slowly trudged through the backyard, taking twice as long to get to Mom's office as it should have. I mulled outside the door for a few minutes and was just about to raise my fist when she opened it.

"What are you doing?" she asked me.

"What?"

"You've been standing out here for five minutes. Are you okay?"

I stared at her blankly. "I need to talk to you about something."

A brief look of concern washed over Mom's face before she quickly composed herself to look professional. "Come inside."

I walked into the office and sat down on the couch closest to the door. Mom sat beside me. I didn't say anything, just looked down at my thighs. I could feel her staring at me.

"So what's on your mind?" she asked. I still didn't say anything. I couldn't remember ever failing anything before. I didn't know how she was going to react. "Aria?" Mom reached out and lifted my chin with her fingertips so I was looking at her.

"I failed my chemistry test this week." I looked down at the ground. "I'm sorry. I need you to sign it."

"I see." Mom's voice was calm. I still couldn't look at her. "Were you prepared for it?"

"I studied really hard Mom, honest I did. Chemistry's just really hard this year and I don't know what's wrong with me."

"Aria!" Mom exclaimed. "There is nothing wrong with you. Look, if you think you did your best then we can talk to Quinn and see if she wouldn't mind helping you with your chemistry until the semester is over."

"She said she would." I closed my eyes and breathed.

"Well there we go," Mom said. "Then that's what we will do. Relax, my darling! It will be okay."

I didn't recognize this woman in front of me. No lecture, no talk about spending too much time with Matt, nothing about time management. Just an as-long-as-you-tried speech. I hadn't been trying as hard as I could; she had to know that. Why was she being so easy on me?

"Aria, are you okay?"

"Me?" I looked at her. "I'm fine."

"Okay." She looked me over very carefully and then chose to believe me. "Well, I need to finish up some work; I'll see you at dinner?"

I stared at her, completely bewildered. I couldn't believe she was just letting this all go.

"Sure," I said, standing up and walking towards the door. "See you at dinner." I closed the door behind me and walked back to the house. One thing was for sure, I definitely didn't know what had happened to my mother.

Dinner that night was tense. I wasn't eating much. Quinn was shoveling food into her mouth before going to work the night shift at the hospital, and both Mom and Robert were unusually quiet.

Finally Robert said something. "So how's school going, Aria?" I almost choked on my stir fry. I looked over to see Mom staring off into space, and then over at Quinn. Quinn shrugged at me.

"It's okay," I said. I didn't really know where the conversation was headed.

Robert raised his dark eyebrows at me. "Your Mom tells me you failed a test?"

"Oh did she?" I asked darting my eyes over to look at Mom, who still was avoiding eye contact. Weird.

"Chemistry?" he prodded.

"I guess so." I dropped my fork on the table.

"You guess so, or you did?" he asked. I felt his dark eyes trying to drill into my mind.

"I did," I said firmly. Then I looked directly into his eyes. "What's it to you?"

Mom snapped back reality. "Aria, watch it," she warned.

"You seem to be spending a lot of time out of the house," Robert said. "Your mother and I are concerned you aren't spending enough time on your studies." Your mother and I. Really? What the heck was his game? I sat there and began to fume. I had a short temper already, but when provoked, it was like a wild fire.

"My mother didn't mention that to me this afternoon," I said coolly. Now Robert looked confused. He looked over to Mom and then back at me.

"You seem to be spending a lot of time with other things these days," he said again. In that moment, I hated him more than ever. "It's really important that you -"

And then I lost it. I stood up from the table, pushing my chair back hard into the wall.

"You're not my father," I said loudly. Very loudly. Too loudly. I could feel my face burning. "It's great that you think you can come in here and try to have a place in my life, but you can't."

"I'm just trying to-"

"I don't give a crap what you are trying to do, Robert." I wasn't about to let him finish his sentence. "You aren't my dad. I haven't even known you for a year. I'm 17 years old. I don't need another parent. I'm almost done. So if you could get off your high horse and go play concerned cop to someone else, that would be swell."

"Aria!" Mom stood up. "Apologize. Now!"

"Don't talk to me," I said. "Screw you. Screw both of you." I walked away from the table and ran out of the house.

I got about halfway down the driveway when I realized I didn't know where I was going. Matt wasn't home. I could go to Callie's. I was panting hard. My mind was going a thousand miles a minute. I had never in my life raised my voice to mom, or any other adult figure to be honest. I didn't know what had just come over me back there. Part of it scared me; the other half of me liked the rush.

I fell to my knees on the grass and started to cry. Tears streamed down my face gently at first, and then I began to sob. I heard the front door open behind me, followed by light footsteps running across the lawn. A pair of arms wrapped around me.

"Let's go inside," Quinn whispered in my ear.

My body started to shake. I didn't know what was happening to me. "I can't go back in there," I finally mustered. Quinn's strong arms lifted me up on my feet. She firmly grasped my arms and led me back into the house. I was shaking uncontrollably as she walked me upstairs to my room. Robert and Mom were nowhere to be seen.

Quinn sat me down on my bed. "How do you feel?" she asked.

"I feel like I can't breathe."

"Are you trying to be metaphorical?" she joked. I glared at her through my tears. "Too soon. Sorry. Okay, I need you to take some deep breaths with me." Quinn slowly counted out 10 deep breaths and I breathed slowly.

"Focus on your breathing," she said, taking my pulse and feeling my forehead. I felt a lot better when we got to 10.

"What was that?" I asked her.

"I think you were having a bit of a panic attack." She got up and handed me a bottle of water that was on my desk. "Drink this." I did as she said.

"So how much trouble am I in?"

"I think it will be okay."

"How? I just told off Mom and my step-father. Nowhere in the world does the concept of that scenario seem okay."

Quinn sighed. "I talked to them for you."

"You did?"

"Yes." She sat down on the bed beside me.

"Why?"

Quinn smiled at me. "Because you're my sister, because I love you. I don't know, Aria. I don't like seeing you like this. You're in a hard spot. I'm older than you – it's different for me. Robert isn't waltzing into my life trying to be my dad. You're almost grown up, but not quite."

"You didn't have to do that," I said. I closed my eyes and fell backwards on the bed.

Quinn flopped down beside me. "You're welcome."

"Thank you."

"So what are we going to do with you?" Quinn grinned at me. "The new family rebel."

I sighed. "I just lost control. I really didn't mean to."

"I know." Quinn sat back up and looked down at me. "Aria?"

"Yes?" I sat back up as well.

"You aren't trying. You're being selfish. Dad would want you to try harder." Her words stung me like disinfectant seeping into a fresh cut. Tears poured down my face once again.

"I didn't mean -"

"Shh," Quinn said, pulling me into a hug and slowly rocking me back and forth. "I know you didn't. It's okay."

I didn't feel okay. I felt out of place in my own home. I just wanted to curl up in a box and never come out. I closed my eyes, pretending that Quinn's arms around me were Matt's. Slowly, I began to feel better.

8.

I woke up around noon the next day. I hadn't slept well the night before; I kept dreaming about Mom, Dad and Robert. I was on trial and Robert was a judge, sentencing me to life in prison. Mom was crying and Dad just looked at me with these sad eyes. Dad hadn't been in my dreams for months, so it was all the more discomforting seeing him look so disappointed in me.

My phone buzzed from across the room. I got out of bed to look at it and saw that it was a text message from Matt. "I miss U. Can't stop thinking of U. 2 more sleeps till I see U again." I smiled.

I stayed in my room for as long as possible. I showered and changed. I even cleaned and did all of my homework that was due next week. Finally, I could smell the delicious scent of turkey and hear a mumble of voices downstairs.

My bedroom door opened and Mom popped her head in. "Robert's parents are here. Can you please come say hello?" I nodded at her. She opened the door all the way. She looked gorgeous, wearing a tight black cocktail dress, her blonde hair pulled up in an elegant knot.

"Mom?" She shot me a look as if to say, 'What now?'

"Yes?"

"You look beautiful." I gave her a small smile.

"Thank you." She ushered me out the door and began walking towards the stairs.

"I'm sorry," I said. She turned around.

"I'm not the one you need to be apologizing to," she said firmly. "Look Aria, I just want to get through dinner right now, okay? So can you please come downstairs and be the pleasant, lovely girl your father and I raised you to be? We can talk about the rest of it later."

"Okay," I said. Time to get this over with.

I had only met Robert's parents three times. Once at the engagement party, next at the rehearsal dinner and again at the wedding. They were nice enough. I never had grandparents growing up. Both of my parents' parents had died before I was born.

"You okay?" Quinn asked me as I joined by her side in the living room.

"Better," I replied. I was going to stay glued to Quinn for the rest of the night, that much was certain. "Is Jeremy coming for dinner?"

"He'll be here soon."

Hugs were exchanged and small talk was made. Quinn shared how her internship was going, Robert talked about an upcoming case he was considering accepting, and even I chimed in with some talk about school and the basketball team. Half an hour later, Jeremy showed up just in time for dinner. I adored Jeremy. He was smart, funny, cute *and* a doctor; Quinn had definitely picked a winner. I sat between Jeremy and Quinn on the couch while Jeremy began to dig at me for information about Matt. A short while later, Mom called us into the dining room for dinner.

We all sat around the table, silent for a minute before Mom spoke. "We have a tradition in our family," she said, "where we all go around the table and say what we are thankful for."

"That sounds lovely, Maggie," Robert's mother said.

"It does," Robert smiled. "I'll go first. I'm thankful for my new family. I know that it's been an adjustment for all of us with the move, but I'd like to thank you all for sticking together and giving me a chance." There was silence.

"Aria," Mom said, "why don't you go next?"

I bit my lip. I felt my heart pounding and heard Quinn's voice in my head saying, "Dad would want you to try harder." I didn't care. I didn't care if she thought I was being selfish. I was angry. I was hurting.

"I'm thankful for…" My voice trailed off. I looked directly at Robert. He raised his eyebrows at me. I looked down at my empty plate, unsure of what to say. I could feel Mom's eyes burning a hole through me.

"I'm thankful for this beautiful turkey and the beautiful people I get to share it with," Jeremy's voice interrupted the silence. He laughed and I followed his lead, when no one was looking I mouthed a silent "thank you" at him. He nodded.

We skipped the rest of the "Thanks" and dug into a delicious turkey dinner. There was conversation, laughter and smiles; overall, it wasn't as horrible as I had anticipated. After dinner, the men turned on the TV to watch football and the ladies sat in the kitchen, sipping on wine. I was excluded from the circle of wine, so I put on my jacket and went outside to get some air.

I sat on the porch swing in the backyard and rocked it back and forth. The door opened and Robert came out.

"Hi," he said.

I wrapped my jacket tightly around me. "Hi."

"Can I sit?"

"It's a free country."

He ignored my jab and pulled a cigar out of his pocket. "Do you mind?"

"Nope." I raised my eyebrows. "I didn't know you smoked."

"Only three a year," he explained.

"Thanksgiving, Christmas and your birthday?" I couldn't help it, I laughed.

"You got it." He lit up the cigar and slowly puffed. "I wanted to talk to you about last night."

I scuffed the ground with the toe of my shoe. "Okay."

Robert inhaled his cigar and let out a long exhale before speaking. "I shouldn't have raised my temper with you the way I did. I'm sorry."

"Really?" I looked up at him.

"I've never done this whole parent thing before, Aria," he said. "Honestly, I have no idea what I'm doing. Here I am with one full-grown step-daughter and another almost grown." Almost grown. I laughed. He made it sound like raising barn animals.

"Well thanks," I told him.

"You're welcome," he said, puffing again. He looked at me expectantly. I knew that look. He was waiting for my apology. I had no desire or intention of apologizing to Robert.

"I'm not trying to replace your dad." As soon as he said those words, it was as if a huge wall between us suddenly evaporated.

"I know," I said. But a part of me still didn't believe him.

"I know I'll never be your dad, Aria," Robert said. "But I do need you to go easier on me."

I didn't know what he wanted me to say. I just sat there, staring at the big oak trees in the back yard. A few minutes later, he stood up.

"I'm going back in," he said. "You coming?"

"Soon," I grunted. I sat there a while longer, rocking back and forth on the porch swing, trying to clear my mind. When my fingers and toes were numb with the fall chill, I retreated back inside.

Closer to midnight, I was reading at my desk when Mom knocked on my door. "Hi," she said.

"Hey, Mom." I closed my book.

"Can I talk to you?"

"If I said 'no,' would you listen?" I teased. She almost looked relieved.

"Well, someone seems to be back to her old snarky self." I pretended to look around the room and she laughed. "When does Matt get back?"

"Monday morning."

"Do you miss him?"

"A ton," I said. "It's weird when you're used to seeing someone everyday…" I let my sentence trail off when I realized who I was talking to.

"Being alone isn't fun," Mom commented, "even if it's only for a few days." That's when it hit me. I don't even know how, but I realized that maybe Mom wasn't so off-base. Sure, her marriage to Robert had been fast, but when you're used to being with someone for so long and then suddenly are left alone – I couldn't even imagine the pain something like that would bring.

"I'm really sorry Mom…" I held back for a moment before finishing my sentence. "…for everything."

She shook her head at me. "I'm starting to see a pattern of apologies with you."

"Maybe because I keep screwing up."

Mom walked over to my bed and sat down. "It's been a hard few months. Robert told me about your talk. I think you owed him an apology." I didn't say anything.

Mom looked at me with these sad eyes. "I wish you wouldn't be this way," she said.

"What way?" My eyes shifted away from her but I already knew what she was talking about.

Mom sighed. "I don't understand why you keep pushing me away."

Is that what I was doing?

"I'm not pushing you away," I told her, but I knew I was.

"Aria –"

"I don't want to talk about Dad," I said, cutting her off. I pursed my lips.

"You can't walk around in an imaginary world," Mom pointed out.

"I'm fine."

Mom reached out for me and I pulled away. I turned my body to look at her. The pain in her eyes was hard to miss. She looked like I had taken a weight and dropped it on her heart.

"We used to be so close," Mom remarked.

"We still are."

"It's not the same," she said softly.

"Well, people change," I huffed. I felt myself getting angry again.

"Is that what you think?" Mom studied my face. "That I've changed?"

"Haven't you?"

She didn't say anything. This was not a common Mom characteristic. Silence was unheard of. She sat there staring at me, like she had no idea who I was; for the first time in my life, I felt the same way about her.

After a few minutes I said I was tired and pushed her out of my room. She looked defeated and upset but chose not to dig any deeper with me. I crawled into bed, trying to ignore to stench of guilt that lingered around me and forget about everything bad in my life.

On Monday afternoon, Matt got home from Victoria. He drove over the second they got in. I was up in my room and could hear him downstairs talking to Mom and Robert. I looked out the window, saw his truck and sprinted down the stairs.

"Hey beautiful," he greeted me.

"Hey yourself." I ran into his arms, he picked me up and spun me around the room. Then he gathered me in his arms and kissed me on the lips.

"Think we could give them a run for their money?" I heard Robert ask Mom in the background.

"Bite your tongue!" she laughed.

"So I have something for you," Matt said, after I pulled him into the living room away from everyone.

"What's that?"

He kissed me.

"Good present," I mumbled. I was in complete bliss.

He pulled a bracelet out from his pocket. "This is for you." I looked at the bracelet as he put it on my wrist. It was silver with a heart link in the middle.

"It's beautiful," I finally said. "I love it."

"And I love you," he said.

I coughed.

"Sorry?"

"I love you, Aria," he said. "I know it's only been two months, but being with you these last two months have been the best two months of my life."

"I love you too," I squealed. He kissed me again. I could feel the magic burning from my lips all the way down to my toes. Matt Lawson loved me. Callie would go nuts when I told her.

"I've never told anyone that before," Matt admitted.

"Neither have I."

"I'm glad."

"So am I." I took his hand and led him into the living room where we spent the afternoon entwined in each other's arms watching old movies on TV and exchanging kisses as often as possible until Mom or Robert popped in to make sure we were coming up for air.

9.

Halloween was quickly approaching in Jordan Falls. I had never really been that into Halloween at home. I mean I had gone trick-or-treating growing up and all that but the older I got the less it stuck. Callie had informed me that Halloween in Jordan falls was a huge deal. We were having a huge Halloween dance at the school, followed by an after party off of school grounds.

Halloween was the talk of the school after Thanksgiving. The decorations went up, dance tickets went on sale and chatter of costumes floated through the school hallways. No one was as excited about the Halloween dance as Callie was. It was all she could talk about. Connor had asked her to the dance, which she kept stressing was strictly a friendship agreement. She did seem to be out of her Logan funk, though, and was excited for the four of us to go together. What were we going to wear? How were we going to get there? Should we all go as some sort of theme? Thank goodness for me both Matt and Connor had immediately deflected her couple-theme idea.

I was too preoccupied with my chemistry homework to think much about anything else. Halloween was on the last Friday of the month, and my chemistry test was the day before. I studied with Quinn every day she wasn't at the hospital. On the side, Quinn had made up practice tests for me to do on my own.

I wasn't seeing Matt as much as I liked, but I needed this test to pull my grade up, and he understood that. Every day after basketball practice, he drove me to the library in town so I could study. Then, about two hours into my study session, he would stop by to say hello and bring me a coffee or tea, then drive me home when I was finished. He made me feel more safe and secure than I ever felt in my entire life.

Things at home were another story. Robert was away again, so I didn't have to worry about him being around. I had been avoiding Mom ever since Thanksgiving and she knew it. She poked her head into my room each night before she went to bed and I always pretended to be asleep. I saw Quinn often and assumed she was feeding Mom reports on my well-being.

The night before my chemistry test, I was at the library doing some last-minute studying with Quinn. The Jordan Falls library was directly across from the pharmacy. Quinn was explaining an organic chemistry problem to me when my eyes darted out the window across the street.

"Aria!" Quinn yelled, interrupting my people-watching and waving her arms. "Your test is tomorrow. Are you even listening?"

"Sorry," I said sheepishly. I took the pencil from her and wrote out the answer to the last half of the problem. "Is that right?"

Quinn looked over my work. "Yeah is it! Good job. I think you are going to be fine tomorrow."

I smiled. "Well, I've had a good teacher."

Quinn rolled her eyes. "You are such a suck up. It's getting late, should we head home?" She closed the textbook in front of us.

"Sounds good to me." I began to pack up my things.

"Hey," Quinn stopped suddenly. "There's Matt." She pointed across the street to the pharmacy. "Who's that guy?"

I looked to where she was pointing. Matt was standing with a guy that I had to squint to make out. He was tall, strongly built, dressed in all black clothes and wearing sun glasses – even though it was night time. Then I realized who it was.

"That's Logan," I shrugged. "He and Matt used to be best friends. Matt told me he was hanging out with some of the guys from the team tonight. I didn't even know they still spoke."

"Weird," Quinn said. "He looks angry." She meant Logan and boy, did he ever. I stared at them across the street; they seemed to be having an intense conversation. Logan looked as though he was getting angrier by the minute. He leaned in towards Matt. Matt raised his hands and walked away.

"Yeah," I replied, feeling puzzled. "He does."

10.

The next morning I woke up feeling fully confident that I was going to do well on my chemistry test. I dressed "for success," as I liked to call it, in a black skirt, purple collared shirt, black blazer and knee-high black leather boots. I still felt nervous, though.

I walked downstairs to the kitchen. Quinn was sitting at the table and let out a wolf whistle. "Hot stuff!" she called out.

"Thanks!" I grabbed a grapefruit and a knife off the kitchen counter.

"Do you feel ready?" Quinn asked.

"I'm nervous," I admitted. I sliced the grapefruit in two pieces and scooped out a small bite with a spoon.

"Don't be nervous, Aria. You know your stuff and will do great."

"I hope so." I pushed the grapefruit to the side, too nervous to eat any more.

Quinn's cell phone buzzed on the counter. She opened it and sighed heavily.

"What's wrong?" I asked.

Quinn tried to hide the worry on her face, but her voice gave it away. "Jeremy and I are just having a bit of a disagreement."

"What? You mean Jeremy did something wrong?" I teased.

"No. He did nothing wrong; it's all me this time."

"What do you -"

"Do you need a ride?" Quinn interrupted, grabbing her bag off the floor. "I need to go to the hospital anyways. I can drop you off."

I glanced at my phone. I hadn't heard from Matt yet; he usually called me in the morning if he was going to pick me up. "Sure, Quinnie," I said, still wondering what her deal with Jeremy was. I decided not to push it; Quinn didn't respond well to pushiness. "A ride would be great."

"We have to go now, then!"

"Sure." I quickly grabbed my stuff and followed her out of the house.

On the way to school Quinn quizzed me on my chemistry knowledge one last time. We didn't talk about anything else the whole way, which was unusual but she seemed distracted. I felt ready to go when she dropped me off.

"Hey, Quinn?" I opened the car door.

"Hey!" She shot back.

I smiled. "Thanks for being awesome."

"Right back at you sister. Now go kick some chemistry butt." She shooed me out of the car and sped away.

The test was pretty easy. I was surprised at how much I had retained in the last few weeks. I felt solid about most of my answers; in fact, I was only unsure of one question. I handed in my test and felt a huge weight lift off my shoulders.

I had fitness next period with Callie. She and I walked down the hallway towards the gym.

"So what are you going to be for Halloween tomorrow night?" Callie asked.

"Ugh." I smacked my hand to my forehead. "Halloween. I don't know Cal – what are you going as?"

"I'm going as a nurse."

"I'll probably just throw something together." I pushed open the change room door and walked inside. "I told you I'm not really that into Halloween and Matt's not either."

"But you guys are still coming to the after party, right?"

"Yeah. At least that's the plan. I haven't seen Matt since yesterday afternoon."

"Trouble in paradise?" Callie teased.

I frowned. "No. I was just at the library with Quinn last night and then I didn't see him this morning."

"Weird," Called remarked. "Usually he follows you around like a lost puppy. Hey, should we hit up the weight room today? Or just throw the ball around?"

"Let's do weights today."

Fitness was a self-instructed class. We got to check in with our teacher at the beginning, who was Coach Matthews, so that gave us an upper hand. We were basically allowed to do whatever we wanted for the remainder of the period as long as it was active. Lately Coach had Callie and I in her office running over practice drills and plays with us.

We exited the change room and went straight into the weight room. "Let's bike first." Callie stated, walking over to the cardio area.

Jordan Falls had the most incredible high school gym I had ever seen. It was an athletics-based school with teams competing nationally for baseball, soccer, basketball, swimming and track and field, and I think there was even a dance team. I'm guessing people didn't have much else to do in a small town but be active or do drugs, and none of us seemed to be on the drugs boat. Because of this sports craze, it meant we had some top-notch workout equipment for training.

Fitness class passed quickly and then we had lunch. I spotted Matt in the cafeteria sitting at a table with a bunch of the guys. I walked over to him.

"Hey there."

"Hey yourself," he said, pulling me towards him and planting a kiss on my lips.

"I missed you this morning," I said.

"Sorry," he said carefully. "Mom needed me to drive the rug rats to school."

"That's okay. What did you get up to last night?"

"Oh not much, just hung out mostly. How did your test go?" I shrugged off his indirect answer to my question.

I smiled at him. "I think it went really well and I feel confident about it. Quinn saved my life."

Matt grinned. "That's awesome, babe. So, I hear we need to figure out some costumes for this Halloween thing tomorrow night."

"Apparently, unless you want to deal with the wrath of Callie."

He made a goofy face at me. "I think I'll pass."

"We'll figure something out," I said with a smile. He leaned forward and kissed me on the lips. "What was that for?"

He grinned. "I just miss you. I haven't seen you very much this week. Is that a problem?" He kissed me again.

"No complaining over here."

"Good. Hey, let's get out of here until next period. Go take a walk or something." He grabbed my hand and I followed him out of the cafeteria. We found a spot outside on the bleachers of the soccer field and stayed there cuddling and kissing until the lunch period ended. I remember in that moment thinking that nothing in my life had ever felt as right as it did with Matt.

11.

On Halloween afternoon I raced home from school with Callie. Matt had to stay after with some of the guys to help move stuff for the dance. Callie had been restless all afternoon, wanting to go home and get ready for the night. I was ecstatic. I got my chemistry mark back that day and ended up with an A minus. Quinn rejoiced with me over the phone. Needless to say, nothing in the world that could bring me down today. Not even a lame Halloween dance.

"So I'll come over after dinner," Callie told me for the millionth time that day. "I'll help you get ready and then Connor and Matt will pick us up."

"Okay Cal," I said, shaking my head at her. "I'll see you later." I ran up the front steps and let myself into the house. I needed to find a costume, but what?

I threw my backpack on the ground and began walking through the house. "Quinn?" I hesitated. "Mom?"

"In here!" Mom called from the living room. I found her sitting on the couch flipping through old photo albums. "How was your day?" she asked as I entered the room. I told her about my test and she commended me on a job well done. "I haven't seen you in a while. Where have you been hiding?"

"The library," I said before changing the subject. "What are you doing?" I sat down on the edge of the couch.

"Oh, I was just looking through some old pictures of you and Quinn on Halloween." I peered over to see the pictures. There was Quinn dressed like a cowgirl and me wearing a big orange pumpkin costume.

Mom smiled at me. "You two were so cute. This was your first Halloween."

"Why are you looking at these?" I cringed.

"Just wanted to see my little babies," she said. "You two have grown up so fast. This feels like just yesterday."

"Right," I shook my head at her. "Hey Mom, do you have anything I can wear to the Halloween dance tonight?"

"I'm sure I can find something from high school," she said.

"That would work. The 80s were golden."

"That they were," Mom smiled. "So this dance is at the school?"

"Yup. Callie's coming over after dinner and then Matt and Connor are picking us up. We are probably going to head over to a party after too."

Mom raised her eyebrows. "Party? Where?"

"Not sure." I gave her a golden smile. "Some kid from school?"

"Chaperones?"

"I'm sure there will be."

"Hm." She looked skeptical.

"Come on Mom. Don't you trust me? It's just a Halloween party. I'll be home by curfew."

"No drinking," she said. "No sex or drugs either."
Her facial expression was dead serious. I burst out
laughing.

"I don't think you have anything to worry about." I
kissed her on the cheek. "Thanks Mom, you're the
greatest."

"Yeah, yeah, mother of the year." She closed the
photo album. "Now let's go find you some clothes."

Mom and I had a blast looking through her old
clothes. It felt like old times again, pre-Robert times. I
ended up dressing in a pair of leggings, some bright lime
green leg warmers and one of the ugliest sequin pattern
shirts I had ever seen in my life. I put my hair up in a side
ponytail and wrapped a headband around my forehead.

"You look cute," Mom said.

"I look like I should go instruct an aerobics class."

She laughed. "That too." The doorbell rang and
Mom went to go let Callie in and I followed.

"Ahhhhh!" Callie shrieked when she saw me. "Aria
you look amazing!"

Callie looked a tad slutty in a white nurse's dress
that showed way too much of her cleavage and didn't cover
enough of her legs. I could see Mom eyeing Callie up and
down with disapproving eyes.

"Thanks, so do you. Come upstairs with me, I need
to do my makeup."

30 minutes later, I was wearing a thick coat of
blush, glitter and the brightest hot pink lipstick I could find.
I found some fake eyelashes in Quinn's room and put those

on as well. Matt and Connor showed up, Connor dressed like a marine and Matt in his baseball uniform.

"How original," Callie grumbled, pointing at Matt's costume.

"What, a baseball player?" Matt asked. "It's classic."

"It's what you wear half the year!" She protested.

"It's hot," I said with a grin. "I like it."

Matt brushed his lips across mine. "Well, that's all that matters. Let's get out of here."

Connor was driving his beat up blue Reliant K. The car groaned and plunked most of the way to school. I was starting to wonder if we would get stranded on the side of the road somewhere. When he parked at the school I literally jumped out of the car.

"I should have warned you about Connor's car," Matt laughed. "It's ride-at-your-own-risk."

"Old Trixie's amazing!" Connor protested as he stepped out onto the sidewalk. "It hurts me that you would say such a thing."

"I think it's ridiculous that your car has a name," Callie said.

Connor rolled his eyes. "Girls. They just don't get it, do they, Lawson?"

"I don't know what you're talking about, Connor." Matt took my hand and we walked away from Connor and Callie towards the school.

The school gym looked like your typical Halloween scene. Black lights, pumpkins, weird things hanging from the ceiling making noises that sounded like a dying dog and blaring music that made me imagine a zombie chasing someone through a cemetery.

I looked around the gym and turned to Matt. "So this is the dance? Pretty cliché if you ask me."

"Dance with me?" Matt asked, but he didn't wait for me to answer and led me out to the dance floor.

"I didn't know you danced," I told him.

"There are a lot of things you don't know about me, Aria," Matt's eyes twinkled mysteriously. I rolled my eyes at his lame line. He spun me around and twirled me back into his arms.

"Where'd you learn?" I asked.

"Summer camp," he laughed. "Who knew they taught dancing at church camp. Of course we weren't allowed to do this." He pulled me into a long embrace and kissed me. When our lips parted, I felt dizzy, like the entire room was spinning.

"I don't know how I found you," I whispered, resting my head lightly on his shoulder.

"I love you, Aria." He responded, kissing my forehead. "You are perfect."

"I love you too." I felt radiant, like I was literally glowing. We stayed that way in each other's arms for a while, swaying to the beat of the music.

The after party was out of control. If Mom had been there, I probably would have been grounded for the next 25 years. You could hear the music blaring from down the street before Connor even pulled up to the house. Inside, people were dancing everywhere, doing keg stands and running around looking like they belonged in a circus.

"I'm not so sure about this," Matt called to Connor.

"Me neither," I turned to look at Callie. "Whose house is this anyways?"

"No idea," she shrugged. Excellent. My nerves were already beginning to shake. We began to walk around the house. Loud techno music pounded into my eardrums like a chain saw. Half way round of the party, I had already seen two girls crying, one throwing up, one guy trying to jump off the roof outside into the pool (a real winner there), one couple who looked like they were about to get into a fist fight and another who looked like she would need to be standing in line for a pregnancy test the next morning. Parties definitely were not my scene.

"This is nuts." A look of concern crossed over Matt's face as he spoke, and I saw worry lines appearing on his forehead. A group of guys approached us. My eyes almost bulged out of my head when I saw Logan leading the pack.

"Lawson, how's it going?" Logan walked up to Matt and shook his hand.

"Not too bad man," Matt gave him a forced smile. "Hey Aria, have you met Logan?" I shook my head in response.

Logan's eyes looked me up and down. "Nice to meet you."

I studied his appearance. He was dressed in all black and his dark eyes looked like sunken black holes. He almost would be attractive if he wasn't trying to be Marilyn Manson's groupie, but there was something else about him that reminded me of the kind of guy you didn't want to end up with in a dark alley.

I glanced at Callie who was suddenly clinging tightly to Connor's arm. I almost snickered at this; so much for her "just friends" speech. Her eye's looked like they could have set Logan on fire.

"Callie," Logan said softly.

Matt put his arm around me. "Aria's my girlfriend." I knew he was trying to deviate the conversation from a possible eruption.

"Good for you," Logan took a swig of his beer. "Want a beer, Lawson?"

Matt held up his hands. "I'm good. Thanks though, man."

"What about you? You want a beer?" Logan held one out to me. I stared at it for a split second.

"No," I said quickly. I didn't have a death wish. My mother had the nostrils of a bloodhound. It was bad enough I was even around beer.

"I thought you didn't drink," Callie said angrily, looking at Logan.

"People change." Logan chugged the rest of his beer and popped open another one. "Catch you guys later."

Callie stormed off in the other direction. "I should probably go see if she's okay," I told the guys.

113

"I'll go," Connor said.

I hesitated. "Are you sure?"

"Very." Connor gave me a close-lipped smile. "We'll find you guys later." He walked off.

"What do you say we go find somewhere where we can be alone?" Matt asked, motioning towards the front door.

I'd say that beat the bleeding eardrum music and the alcoholic chimpanzees around me.

After finding Callie and making sure she was as okay as she could be, we ended up leaving the party and decided to walk home. It wasn't that far and it was still early. "Let's go this way," Matt said. He turned down a street.

"Sure," I told him. I had no idea where we were. We ended up down by the lake. He led me towards the forest. "Are you taking me out here to kill me?" I joked.

Matt laughed. "No, I want to show you something."

I sighed. "Of course you do. No offence, Matt, but it's Halloween and a guy leading a girl into the woods is a little creepy. Especially when you've read like a million horror stories that result in hooks hanging from trees and axe murders."

"Relax!" He squeezed my arm. "You are safe with me."

"So tell me about Logan," I said as we walked together.

"What about him? He's Callie's ex. I already told you that."

I narrowed my eyes at him, even though it was dark and he couldn't see. "Callie told me you and Logan used to be best friends."

"Used to, meaning past tense." Matt was holding out on me and I didn't know why.

"What happened? I heard about the accident with his brother."

"He just blew me off." I could hear the hurt in Matt's voice.

"Blew you off? How?"

"He just wouldn't talk to me. Stopped answering his phone and started hanging out with a new group of guys – bad guys. He changed a lot. The guy was my best friend my whole life and then he wanted nothing to do with me."

I took his hand in mine and squeezed it tightly. "I can't imagine how hard that must have been."

"It was."

We walked a few more steps and came to a small house – more like a house for babies or midgets.

"What's this?" I asked.

"It's a clubhouse that Logan and I built when we were growing up." He led me inside and lit a match. The dark room came into view. It was a one-room wooden shack with two windows, a blanket on the floor and a few chairs.

115

"Looks like it's been used?" I remarked.

"I think some of the guys come here sometimes." He lit two candles that were on the floor and I sat down on the blanket beside him.

"What is this, the love shack?" I started laughing.

"No," he said defensively. "It's not like that at all!"

"I was kidding."

"Oh." Matt turned about four shades of purple. There was an awkward silence. "Sorry about the party."

"It's not like you planned it or anything."

"I know. I just don't like being in situations like that. I'm not that kind of guy."

I smiled adoringly at him. "I didn't think you were."

"Come here." He leaned forward and kissed me. The kiss was long. Longer than usual. I felt Matt's body heat electrifying towards mine, like I was on fire. I let my mind drift and I sank into the kiss. I ran my fingers through Matt's hair. He placed his hand on my waist and I barely noticed that it began to wander up towards my chest. He stopped suddenly.

"I'm sorry." He stood up quickly and moved about a foot away from me.

I was unsure how to react. I'd never had a guy want to stop during a makeout session before. "It's okay," I finally said.

"I don't want to move too fast," Matt said. He looked confused. "I just think we need to slow down. Physically, I mean. I'm not ready for…"

"It's okay," I said again. "You don't need to explain. I understand. Slow is a good idea for me as well."

"Good." Matt ran his hands through his light blond hair. I didn't know what to do next. I stood up.

"So should we go?" I asked softly.

"Yeah," he sighed. "We should probably get you home."

I blew out the candles and starting walking towards the door.

"Aria?"

"Yes?"

"You don't think I'm a total loser now, do you?"

I laughed out loud. I couldn't help it. I grinned, although he couldn't see me in the dark room. "If anything, I think I just fell more in love with you."

"Have I told you how awesome you are?" I could hear the relief in his voice. His hand found mine and we walked outside.

"You have," I grinned. "But you can keep telling me. I have no issue with that."

He kissed my nose. "I love you."

"I love you too."

The walk home was freezing. I swear it felt like it was going to snow soon. Matt said it was too early for snow, but I could smell the scent of icicles in the air. He laughed at me and said no one could smell snow. I disagreed.

I got home just before midnight with minutes to spare before my curfew. I shivered as a let myself into the house and decided to make myself a cup of tea before bed.

Mom was sitting as the kitchen table with a mound of paperwork in front of her, typing away on her laptop.

"Hey," I said. I walked over to the stove, grabbed the kettle and began filling it with water.

"Hi, sweetheart," Mom adjusted her glasses. "How was your night?"

"Oh, it was good." I set the kettle on the stove. "Is Quinn home yet?"

"She's still at work. I talked to her a while ago; she's working overtime now. She said she would be home soon."

I scrunched my nose. "Halloween at the hospital would probably be a nightmare."

"She said it was insane," Mom said with a wince. "So how was the party?"

"Meh." I shrugged. "Kind of lame I guess. We were only there for 20 minutes. It was a little out of control."

A worried look appeared on Mom's face. "What happened?"

"Nothing happened!" I sat down beside her. "Just lots of drinking and Matt didn't want to be at a place like that, so we left."

"Well that was very responsible of you," Mom remarked. Gold star for Matt. "So what were you doing until now?"

I felt my cheeks begin to heat up. "Oh you know, just hanging out at the lake."

Mom looked skeptical. "Just hanging out?" She echoed a teasing voice back at me.

"Yup." The kettle started to whistle. Saved by the bell. I walked back over to it and turned my back to her.

"Just be careful, Aria." Mom almost whispered this as if I wasn't supposed to hear it.

I turned and smiled at her. "Matt's a good guy."

"And you've got a good head on your shoulders," Mom shut her laptop. "But you're my baby and I still worry."

I groaned. She kissed me on the forehead.

"I'm going to bed. Good night, honey."

"Good night." I turned back to my tea and slowly began to steep it. When it was ready I padded down the hallway to the living room where I sat on the couch, sipping my tea and thinking about how wonderfully everything was coming along.

Winter

12.

The first snowfall of the school year came the day after school let out for Christmas vacation. I woke up on Saturday morning to find a two-foot thick blanket of pure whiteness covering our entire property. I raced downstairs.

Both Mom and Robert were sitting at the kitchen table typing away on their laptops. What a romantic breakfast. Quinn was at the counter eating a bowl of cereal. She looked like she hadn't slept in days, dark circles looming under her eyes.

"Good morning!" I practically yelled with enthusiasm. Robert shot Mom a suspicious look out of the corner of his eye.

"Good morning, sweetie," Mom said, eyes not moving from the computer screen. The others responded in unison.

"It's snowing!" I raised my voice with excitement.

"It is," Robert observed dryly.

"I had no idea," Quinn raised her eyebrows mockingly at me.

"Jerk." I stuck out my tongue at her. What was with adults and snow? It was like it was the devil or something.

"I hope the roads aren't too bad," Quinn said in a worried tone.

"What time do you need to be at the hospital?" Robert asked.

"About an hour."

"If the roads aren't plowed when you have to leave I can take you in my truck," he said.

"Can you take me to Matt's?" I piped up.

"Aria," Mom looked up from her computer, "I'm not sure I want you going anywhere today. It's miserable outside. And if you go to Matt's, I don't know how you'll get home later if the roads get worse." Robert nodded in agreement.

"I could always stay there," I suggested. Quinn burst out laughing, Robert raised his eyebrows, and Mom shot me a look indicating that was probably the worst idea in the world.

"Good idea, Aria," Quinn nudged me. I grabbed my cell phone and texted Matt, telling him I couldn't get to his house. I was disappointed. It was my first snowfall in Jordan Falls and I wanted to spend it with my boyfriend.

"I was going to decorate for Christmas today," Mom told me. "Want to help?"

I pondered this for a moment. A big part of me wanted to skip Christmas this year. We hadn't had a Christmas in our home last year. Dad had passed away two days before and we had all been much too distraught and isolated to even think about Christmas. It felt better in my mind to not do it again than to have to go through another first holiday. Especially after Thanksgiving had been such a colossal disaster. However, I knew Mom would be hurt if I didn't help her.

124

"Or you could help me put up all the Christmas lights outside," Robert smiled coyly at me. I could see Mom watching me carefully out of the corner of my eye. She knew how hard this holiday was going to be for all of us. The one-year anniversary of Dad's death wasn't going to be easy.

"I'll help, Mom," I said quickly. "When do you want to start?"

"Just let me finish going through these emails," she nodded towards the computer screen. "10 more minutes?"

"Sounds good." I left the kitchen and went upstairs to change. I was staring out my window looking at the snow when my phone rang. It was Matt.

"Hi, beautiful." His voice was deep and soft.

"Hi. What are you doing?"

"I just built a snowman with Ruthie. She is quite the bossy one."

I laughed. "Sounds like fun."

"Now we're making pancakes."

"I wish I was there."

"I wish you were too," he said. "Dad might let me take the ATV's out later, so if he does I'll stop by? He won't let me drive my truck. Apparently the roads are a mess."

"So I've heard."

"Okay babe, I have to go. Ruthie's calling me. I just called to say hi."

"Hi." I grumbled, disappointed that we couldn't talk for longer.

"Hey, don't be grumpy."

"I wanted to see you today," I whined. "It's the first day of Christmas vacation."

"I know babe," he said softly. "But what can you do? We'll figure something out."

"I guess," I said quietly.

"I love you." I could hear him smiling through the phone.

"I love you too."

"I'll call you later, okay?"

"Okay…bye."

"Bye Aria."

I hung up the phone, slightly irritated.

"Aria!" Mom called from the first floor. "Come help me!" I grudgingly dragged myself down the stairs to help her.

I followed Mom through the mountain of snow in the back yard into the garage where we had stored all the Christmas stuff after we moved. Mom, Robert and I carried all the boxes back into the living room.

"All right, ladies," Robert said, placing the last box on the floor. "I'm going to snow blow the driveway and put up the Christmas lights. If you need any help, let me know." He kissed Mom lightly on the lips, shrugged his feet back into his boots and went out the front door.

"Ready?" Mom asked me. "I thought we could start with the tree."

The tree. Last year Quinn had still been at school writing her finals, so Mom, Dad and I had decorated the tree, just the three of us. It was fun and silly. Mom made popcorn and hot chocolate and Dad sang along to Christmas carols. He couldn't sing, so this made it all more amusing. The memory nearly knocked me to the floor.

"Aria, what are you thinking about?" Mom asked me.

I hesitated. "Last Christmas." I couldn't look at her for fear that I would burst into tears. I walked over to the box that held our artificial Christmas tree and began to unfold the box flaps.

"I know it's hard," Mom said. "I've been trying not to think about it either."

"Really?" Coming from Mom the psychologist, not thinking about your emotions usually wasn't an option.

"Yes." Mom took a step toward me and took my hands in hers. "This is going to be a hard week for all of us and that's okay."

"I just kind of wish we could skip Christmas this year."

"Robert offered," Mom told me.

"He did?" I must have looked surprised.

"He knows how hard it will be."

"Really?"

"He's not a bad guy, Aria." As much as I hated to see the truth in that, I was starting to see where she was coming from.

"He's okay." I said this simply to avoid an argument.

She smiled. "I'm glad you think so. Now let's get this puppy ready to go."

Mom and I had fun decorating the tree. It was silly and comfortable – exactly what I needed. Robert came in and the three of us sipped on coffee, then he pulled us outside to show us his work.

Robert had strung white lights that accented the snow all around the house, the porch and down the driveway. It looked magical.

"Wow," I breathed. "This looks awesome, Robert."

"I'm glad you like it," he smiled at me, pleased by the positive reinforcement. I heard a loud noise behind me that sounded like an old car engine. I spun around to find Matt sitting on an ATV parked on the driveway.

"You came!" I squealed, running over to him. He picked me up, spun me around and planted a kiss on my lips.

"I told you we'd figure it out," he grinned. "First snow day, I couldn't miss being with my girl."

I smiled. "That's what I like to hear." Matt's eyes glistened and then he picked me up and threw me in a snow bank.

"Hey!" I protested, wiping the snow out of my now ice cold face. Matt held out his hand to Robert for a high five. "Boys," I muttered as I got up. Mom laughed and helped me brush the snow off my body.

"Want to go for a ride?" Matt asked. My eyes widened and I turned to Mom.

"Can I?" I asked. Mom looked uncertain. She glanced over a Robert who was already inspecting the ATV.

"They are perfectly safe," Robert told her. "My dad and I used to have them growing up."

"Oh, okay," Mom gave in. "Just please be careful. And wear a helmet!"

"Don't worry, I brought an extra," Matt told her. "Dad is big on safety."

"Good man," Robert commented. Matt passed me a helmet and I put it on. I got on the ATV after him, straddling my legs over the seat and wrapping my arms around his middle.

"It's just like riding a horse with an engine," Matt explained.

Mom laughed out loud. "I don't think Aria's even been within 10 feet of a horse!" she said.

"City folks," Robert said, shaking his head. Matt nodded in agreement.

"Have fun!" Mom waved us off. And off we went.

The ATV thrilled and terrified me at the same time. I screamed probably for at least three quarters of the ride and Matt just laughed at me, driving as fast as he dared. We got back to my house an hour later and began building a snow fort in the front yard.

"Hey, Aria?" Matt peered over the big hill of snow between us.

"Yes?"

"I was wondering," he said nervously, "and you can totally say no if you don't want to, but I just thought that maybe you'd want to…" He stopped talking.

"What?" I shot him a look letting him know he was being an odd ball.

"Do you want to come to church with me tomorrow?" He shot the words out of his mouth so quickly it actually came out more as "dyouwannacometourchtomorrow?"

Church. Ugh. I didn't like to think about church anymore. The last time I had set foot in a church was at Dad's funeral last Christmas. When Dad was alive, we had gone to church every Sunday. Mom and Robert still went every week but never forced me to go with them. Part of me thought I still had some unresolved issues with God about Dad's death. I could think of a million other things I'd rather do than sit in a church praising a God I didn't understand.

"Aria?" Matt was staring at me and I realized I hadn't answered his question.

"Of course I'll go to church with you," I heard myself say, then I wanted to curse myself.

"Really?" He smiled the biggest smile I had ever seen. "That's great. My dad said he would pick you up tomorrow on our way."

"Okay." I smiled at him, hoping to hide my urge to dunk my head into the massive pile of snow in front of me.

We were both completely soaked after building an awesome snow fort, so we went inside. Mom gave Matt a pair of Dad's old sweats and sweatshirt and I changed into some of my own. She made us hot chocolate and we spent the rest of the afternoon cuddled together on the couch watching old movies. Of course, this was interrupted by Mom or Robert pretending to look for something every 30 minutes.

Matt stayed for dinner and we helped Mom and Robert cook up a yummy stew. I was pleasant the whole time, answering all of Robert's questions with a smile. We enjoyed our delicious meal and then they kindly suggested it was time for Matt to head home as it was getting dark. I was disappointed, but I respected their decision. It was starting to snow again and Robert wanted him home before the roads got any worse.

I walked him to the door and we kissed goodbye. He said he would see me for church in the morning – a thought I had tried to push out of my mind for the evening.

Robert had gone to pick Quinn up from the hospital, so Mom and I tackled the pile of dishes. Quinn walked into the kitchen looking exhausted. Her long straight blonde hair was in a messy ponytail and she had huge bags under her eyes.

"I'm going to church with Matt tomorrow," I said, putting a glass in the dishwasher.

"That's nice, honey," Mom said, scrubbing a pan in the sink. She glanced at Quinn. "Long day, sweetheart?"

"Extremely long. I'm dead tired." She sat down at the table and looked at me. "You're going where?"

"Church."

"Really?" She looked uncertain as to whether or not I was kidding.

"Yeah," I said uneasily. "Matt asked if I would go."

"But you haven't been to church since…"

"I think it's great," Mom said, interrupting Quinn. "Good for you, Aria." She walked over to Quinn. "Are you feeling alright, sweetie?" She put her hand on Quinn's forehead. "You don't look so good."

Quinn brushed off Mom's hand, "I'm fine Mom. Just tired. Training to be a doctor isn't the easiest job in the world." Mom still didn't look convinced, but went back to her dishwashing.

"Are you seeing Jeremy tonight?" I asked Quinn, "I haven't seen him much lately." Quinn's face sunk and her cheeks turned a scarlet red. She shifted uncomfortably.

"Jeremy and I are taking a bit of a break." Mom dropped the pan she was holding in the sink.

"You're what?" She exclaimed at the same moment I shouted. "Really?"

Quinn sighed. "Yes." She looked at her hand and starting picking at her fingernails.

"Since when?" Mom asked.

"Yesterday."

"Why didn't you tell me?" I asked.

"I don't know. There's not really anything to talk about. Jeremy's really busy in his first year of residency. We work opposite shifts and don't really have time to see each other right now."

"Are you okay?" Mom asked.

"I don't know," Quinn said in a monotone voice. "I've been trying not to think about it."

I was completely shocked. Jeremy and Quinn had been together since I was in eighth grade. I thought they were going to get married some day. "Whose idea was it?" I asked.

"It was mutual. We are going to talk again in a few weeks. We've just been together forever. I don't know. I don't know if I want to be with someone right now." She looked defeated. "I'm going to go have a shower and get some sleep." She left the room.

Mom's eyes followed her. "I'll be right back," she told me. "I just want to go make sure she's okay."

"Good idea." I went back to loading the dishwasher. I knew Quinn and I knew part of her and Jeremy taking a break probably had a lot to do with the upcoming anniversary of Dad's death. Quinn likes to pretend she is invincible, but she also can shut people out when she's hurting.

I picked up the phone and dialed Matt's number. He answered on the first ring. The second I heard his voice I felt calm flow through my body. "Miss me already?"

"You bet I did." I told him about Quinn and Jeremy.

"That's rough, Aria," he said. "I'm sorry." There was a silence for a moment before he spoke again. "Hey, so I was thinking about Monday." Monday was the anniversary of Dad's death. "I'm not sure if you just want to be alone or if you want to do anything. But I was talking to some of the guys tonight and we were all going to go snowboarding if you're interested. I totally understand if you just want to be alone though, or even just want it to be us instead of a group thing."

"Actually, a group thing sounds really great," I told him. "I'm not sure if Mom has anything planned for us as family so I'll have to double check. Snowboarding sounds really fun, although I haven't been much."

"I'll teach you some moves," Matt said in a cocky tone.

"Oh will you?"

"You know it."

That night I was lying in my bed about to fall asleep when I heard a noise coming from the bathroom. At least that's where I thought it was coming from. Quinn and I shared a bathroom that separated our two bedrooms. I walked into the shared space. The door to Quinn's room was closed. I could hear her crying on the other side. I hesitated momentarily before quietly pushing it open, then I tip-toed across her room towards the big mound of blankets which she was under.

"Quinnie?" I whispered.

"Hey," she sat up in bed. I took a look at her blotchy, tear-stained face and sighed.

"You want to talk about it?" I offered.

She shook her head. "Not really. Apparently I'm you at Thanksgiving now." I laughed. I stood there staring at her, unsure of what to do next. She pulled the big comforter over to the side and patted the bed. I crawled underneath the covers with her.

We lay there for a few minutes, both staring at the ceiling when finally Quinn spoke.

"Mom thinks I'm sabotaging my relationship with Jeremy." She sounded slightly annoyed, but more tired. Tired of fighting.

"Are you?"

She sighed. "I don't know. Maybe. Maybe moving here with you guys was a bad idea."

I rolled over on my side to face her. "Quinn, if you hadn't been here with me these last few months I probably would have jumped off a bridge."

A street light from outside shone through the blinds and lightly marked a line across Quinn's face. I saw her smile. "You would have managed."

"No, I wouldn't." I found her hand under the covers. "Quinn, do you know how many times you have talked me out of either running away or smashing someone's head in with a lamp this year?"

She laughed. "Jeremy and I just want different things and we've been fighting all the time. We never used to fight."

"Like what?" I pulled my knees to my chest.

"Oh I don't know. Work, life, family. You know how it is." I didn't. I didn't say anything.

She bit her lip. A habit I had apparently inherited. "I'm afraid."

"Of?" But I didn't even have to ask. I already knew. It was the same reason why I hadn't wanted to get close to Matt. "Losing him," I said. "You're afraid of losing him." She nodded.

I sat up. "I'm afraid too. But I think one of the greatest things about being in love is the fear because with it comes the sheer delight of knowing you are safe and protected. You can't spend your whole life wondering, 'What if?' Look at Mom – she got hurt, she lost Dad and she went looking for love again. She's happy, Quinnie. You need to let yourself be happy."

Quinn lay there for a few minutes. She sat up next to me and stared at me.

"What?" I asked, hesitant.

"I was just trying to remember when you got so smart." She gave me a half smile.

"I think it runs in the family."

"I'm not so sure." Quinn frowned and sunk back down under the covers.

"You'll figure it out." I lay down next to her and closed my eyes tightly.

13.

I woke up early the next morning feeling disoriented. I looked around the room – Quinn's room – and it took me a few seconds to figure out what I was doing in there. I rolled over and glanced at the digital alarm clock on Quinn's nightstand. It was only 7 a.m. I threw her huge down comforter off of my body and walked into our bathroom.

A long hot shower was in order. I turned on the water, stepped inside and tried to drown out my thoughts. Thirty minutes later, I wrapped a towel around my body and stepped out of the tub. Quinn wandered in.

"Hey," I said, reaching for my hair mouse sitting on the counter.

"Morning," she nodded at me. She picked up her brush and ran it through her straight, long blonde hair.

"Work today?"

"Day off."

"You're up early." I shot some mouse into my hand and began to work it through my damp hair.

Quinn shrugged in her massive hoodie that fell to her knees. "Couldn't sleep."

"Have you heard from Jer?" I asked, slowly starting to scrunch my hair. Having curly hair was a pain sometimes.

"He wants to meet for breakfast and talk." Quinn stuck her finger in her mouth and began biting her nails. One of the only bad – and might I add disgusting – habits that she had.

"Relax," I told her, reaching for the gel. "That's a good thing, Quinnie."

"I know." She sighed. "So you are really going to church?"

I shot her an annoyed look. "Why is that so hard to believe? We used to go to church all the time."

"Yeah," she said, "but that was before –"

"It's important to Matt," I interrupted.

Quinn sat down on the edge of the tub. "So you guys are getting pretty serious."

"I love him," I told her without hesitation. I shook my hair loosely and let it fall across my face. I grabbed my mascara and began applying it to my eyelashes.

"He seems like a really good guy."

"He is amazing." I finished my right eye and moved on to my left.

Quinn smiled at me. "I'm happy for you, Aria."

"Thanks Quinnie." I splashed some blush across my cheeks and smacked my lips in the mirror, satisfied with my reflection. "Now on to more important matters. What should I wear?"

With Quinn's help I selected a nice pair of black slacks, a red Christmas-looking shirt and a black cardigan.

"Very nice," Quinn smiled at my final attire.

"Thanks." I looked at the clock. It was only 8 a.m. "Now I only have two hours to kill."

"You know I think I'd actually rather go to church than talk to Jeremy right now." Quinn made a gagging motion.

"You are being a goof." I grabbed her hand and walked her into her bedroom. "Here's what you're going to do. You are going to put on some super hot clothes, glam up a bit and go get your man back."

Quinn looked like her puppy had just been run over by a milk truck. Her lower lip curled into a pout and her eyes brimmed with tears. I tried a gentler approach. "Do you know what you are going to say to him?"

She shook her head in response. "I don't know what I want."

"Just stop thinking about it right now." I walked across the padded carpet towards her large walk-in closet. "Come on; let's find you something to wear."

After getting Quinn ready we both went downstairs to the kitchen. I majorly needed a caffeine fix. Mom was standing over the stove, frying pan in one hand, spatula in the other and wearing an apron – an apron! "I made pancakes," she said, nodding towards a stack of dollar-thin pancakes on the counter.

Quinn and I exchanged "what the heck" glances and stood there staring at our mother. Mom wasn't really the Betty-Crocker-in-the-kitchen type. Not a bad cook, just not the kind that you would see on a Sunday morning cooking breakfast in an apron. I don't think I had ever seen my mother wear an apron.

"Why?" I asked, not in the nicest voice ever.

"Yeah," Quinn frowned. "What's going on?" Mom didn't answer and continued to flutter around the kitchen.

"Where's Robert?" I asked.

"Still sleeping," she replied. "Sit down, have some breakfast." She grabbed the stack of pancakes, put it on the table and then immediately went over to the sink and started washing dishes. It took me about two seconds to realize what she was doing.

Diversion. A lovely family trait passed down from my mother to me and my sister. Mom busies herself when she was upset; Quinn pretends everything is perfect. When I was upset...well, apparently I storm out of the house in a mad rage, but usually I was a combination of the two of them.

"I'm meeting Jeremy for breakfast," Quinn said.

Mom looked up from the pan she was scrubbing. "Are you? That's great sweetheart."

"If by 'great' you mean completely nerve-wracking, then yes."

"It will be fine," Mom soothed.

"I hope so."

I reached for a pancake and shoved it into my mouth. "These are great," I murmured. Both Mom and Quinn turned to look at me. Quinn shook her head.

"I have to go," she said. "Have fun at church, Aria." She grabbed her purse off the counter and walked out the door. I clamped my teeth down hard at the mention of church.

"What time is Matt picking you up?" Mom asked.

"Soon." I poured myself some coffee and took a long sip. "Are you guys going to church today?"

"We sure are," Robert's deep voice boomed as he walked into the kitchen. He kissed Mom gently on the lips. "Good morning, my love. Something smells amazing!" She giggled. I cringed. "Need a ride?" Robert asked.

"Nah," I said. "Matt said his parents would pick me up on their way."

"Sounds good," he said, sitting down next to me and helping himself to some pancakes.

I stared out the glass sliding doors and watched the snowflakes falling lightly from the sky.

Matt's truck pulled into our driveway about 30 minutes before church started. I ran outside to meet him. Ruthie was sitting in the front seat next to her big brother.

"We can't all fit in one car," Matt explained, opening the truck door for me.

I nodded and climbed in. "Hi Ruthie," I smiled down at the little girl. "How's it going?"

"I get to go to Sunday school today," she said.

"That's exciting."

"Matt's my teacher, Matt says you get to teach with him today."

"Oh really?"

"We get to learn about Noah and the animals!" she grinned. She had Matt's dimples. I couldn't help but smile.

"Well I might need your help brushing up on my Noah knowledge, Ruthie. It's been a while since I've gone to Sunday school."

"Daddy reads me stories from the Bible every night," Ruthie babbled. "We learn about Jonah, and Moses, and Jesus, and Daniel! Did you know my name's from the Bible? Ruth!"

I laughed. "I did know that, Ruthie."

"Daddy says Ruth was a strong woman with good character," she said proudly. I gave her what I thought was an affirmative smile.

I was silent the rest of the car ride but listened to Ruthie go on about snow and everything she could think of. When we pulled up to the church, I felt my chest tighten. I took a few slow, deep breaths and tried to compose myself as Matt opened the truck door for me to get out.

The church was small. That didn't really surprise me for Jordan Falls. Everything here was small. The church had an old-fashioned, classic look with white paneling and a small landing in base of the front doors with black metal railings. Like an old church that would pop out at you in a movie or TV show, ironically relaying a calming yet creepy feeling.

The inside was pretty standard. A long aisle separating about 20 rows of pews. At the front was a white tile stage with a large wooden cross at the centre. Matt held my hand which I couldn't help thinking was a good plan. It took a good deal of inner strength not to turn around and run back to the truck.

Matt took me down the aisle to a pew near the front, most of which was already filled with his family members. I waved hello to his parents and siblings, then the service began. Music started playing and we were all asked to stand together and sing. I wasn't much for singing; truth be told, I wasn't very good, but I did my best. I listened as Matt sang a beautiful melody next to me. No surprise there. I had yet to find something he wasn't talented at.

After the singing, the head pastor came on the stage and welcomed everyone, then we sat down. I shifted in the rock-hard pew, not exactly the most comfortable seating arrangement; my guess was they didn't want people falling asleep during the service. We then stood up to shake hands with the people around us. Everyone seemed nice enough, but I couldn't help feeling like people were staring at me and Matt. In a small town, everyone was curious.

The pastor started his sermon after that. He told the story of Jesus healing the paralytic. He talked about having faith. To me, faith was an interesting theory. I understood the idea of believing something without seeing, how people could feel God and all of that. I got that. What I didn't get was why bad things happened to some people and not to others. I knew the Sunday school answers to these questions. About how God had given people free will and that's why bad things happened. I just didn't understand why some people didn't have a choice. Like Dad.

No one killed my father. He died of a heart attack. In my mind, God was the one who killed him. This had lit a raging fire of anger within me. I was mad. I was mad at

God and no one could say anything to change that. No one could explain how or why Dad had died. I remember when it happened how people had told me it was "his time to go." That was the least creative load of crap you could tell a person.

This was why I hated being in church.

I didn't understand how people found church comforting. All these unknown theories you were supposed to just place your beliefs in. My world had been so shattered in the last year, I wasn't sure if even God could pick up the pieces.

So I sat there in the pew with a small scowl on my face. The second Matt shot a glance in my direction, it instantly turned into a radiant smile.

Halfway through the service, Matt took my hand in his and whispered into my ear. "I'm so glad you're here with me." Those words alone were enough to keep me intact until the end of the service. The minute the hour-long service ended, Matt whisked me off to the Sunday school room to get ready for the lesson.

"So what did you think?" he asked. Before I couldn't even think of a response he said what was really on my mind. "You didn't like it, did you?"

I twirled one of my long curls around my finger to hide my nervousness. "It's not that I didn't like it."

"But it's just not your thing?"

"I didn't say that."

"So what are you saying?"

I sighed. "Well if you'd let me speak I'd tell you."

"I'm sorry. This is just really important to me."

"I know that Matt, that's why I'm here." I shook my head. "I liked it. It wasn't bad or anything, but being in a church is still really hard for me. You know that."

His face fell for a moment but his glowing smile was intact when he looked back at me. "Fair enough. I'm still really glad you came."

"Me too." Inside I sighed of relief. "So what do you do for Sunday school?"

He pulled out a teaching booklet and began to walk me through the pages.

The class was actually a lot of fun. It was full of about 20 kids from kindergarten to grade four. Matt was great with the kids. He played games, sang songs and told stories. They all looked at him like he was this amazing guy – which he was – but seeing him with the kids like that made me love him even more. When the class ended I had a big, goofy grin on my face.

"What are you smiling about?" Matt asked me as we walked hand in hand back to his truck.

"Just thinking about how madly in love I am with you."

He stopped in the middle of the church parking lot and gathered me into his arms, softly sweeping his lips across mine. "Funny, I was just thinking that too. Now come on, we've to get back for lunch."

In Matt's family, Sunday lunch was a big tradition. Every Sunday after church his Mom cooked a roast with all the fixings and the whole family ate together.It was a huge gathering. Since Mom had never met them, Matt's parents had invited her and Robert over as well. Rachel and I helped Mom and Carol in the kitchen while Matt, Ruthie, Anna, Adam and Micah played Monopoly in the living room. The two men watched Sunday football in the background.

I loved being part of a big family. So complete. The four of us worked away in the kitchen, exchanging jokes and stories like we were old friends. Mom looked relaxed, which was a relief to me. Her and Carol seemed to get along really well. Everything was going smoothly between our families which helped to ease my anxious nerves. When the food was finally ready, we all gathered around the living room table to eat. We held hands as Peter prayed over our meal.

Dinner was filled with numerous conversations. I spent most of it talking to Rachel about how college was going for her and what my plans were for next year. She was thinking of going into medicine – I told her to talk to Quinn. Matt was busy talking to his dad, Robert and Micah about his future baseball plans.

I loved listening to Matt talk; I could do it for the rest of my life. I sat at the table taking in his voice in complete bliss. I didn't know what I had done to get so lucky. The last few months with Matt seemed so surreal. That night, when he walked me to the door with Mom and Robert, I felt like I was in a heavenly trance.

Matt kissed me on the lips. "So Callie and I will pick you up around 8 o'clock tomorrow morning? Is that okay?"

"Perfect." I snuggled up against him to say goodbye and then followed Robert out to the truck.

"What are you doing tomorrow?" Mom asked me.

"Going snowboarding." I climbed into the back seat of Robert's truck. Mom got in and turned around to face me.

"All day?" she asked.

"Yeah…" I hesitated. "I'm sorry…I meant to ask you about it." She didn't respond for a moment, just stared out the truck windshield. "Mom?"

"Yeah?" she snapped back to reality. "Oh. It's okay…I just thought we'd be together tomorrow."

"I'm in court all day tomorrow," Robert told me.

"Oh…" I felt my stomach begin to tighten and my chest pounded with anxiety. "Well I'll be back in time for dinner Mom. We can have a nice dinner together."

"Okay." The car was filled with silence.

"I can tell Matt I'm not coming if you want?" I offered. "I can stay home with you."

"That's okay." Mom gave me a small smile. "Go have fun with your friends."

"Are you sure?"

"Yes!"

We pulled into the driveway and, seeing Quinn's car, I bolted from Robert's truck and into the house. I was anxious to hear about her morning with Jeremy. I found her in her bedroom sitting at her desk leafing through a medical dictionary.

"Hey!" I called, entering the room.

"Hi." She turned around in her desk chair to face me. "How was church?"

"It was okay I guess," I shrugged. "But Matt was really great teaching Sunday school with all the little kids. They were so cute." I sighed and sat down on her bed.

Quinn laughed. "Man you've got it bad, Aria."

I smiled. "You look like you're feeling better. How was your talk with Jeremy?"

Quinn frowned, "Still unresolved. He's going back to Toronto to be with his family for Christmas. He leaves Christmas Eve and is flying back in a few days after Boxing Day. Then he wants to get together and talk again. 'Give me a few days to think,' he said."

"What's to think about? You two love each other."

"Oh Aria," she said. "It's not that simple. Not everything is black and white."

"Maybe it is." Mom's voice flooded Quinn's room from the doorway where she stood.

"How?" Quinn sounded defeated.

"You need to follow your heart, sweetie. You can't be afraid."

"Did I miss something?" I asked, feeling confused.

Quinn sighed. "Jeremy asked me to marry him."

"He WHAT?" I exclaimed, practically falling off the bed.

"That's why we broke up," Quinn explained. "I said I wasn't ready for that. That's why he wants to talk when he comes home. He wants me to reconsider."

"You knew this?" I said to Mom, who nodded in response. "Does no one tell me anything around here anymore?"

Mom laughed. "Sorry, honey, it wasn't intentional."

"I wasn't ready to broadcast it yet," Quinn said.

"But Quinn, this is Jeremy," I protested. "You've talked about marrying Jeremy since I thought boys should live in a zoo and have a keeper!"

"Things are different now."

"Why do you keep saying that?"

"Because they are." Quinn's voice quivered slightly and her eyes filled with tears. "I don't really want to talk about this anymore."

"But Quinn…"

"Aria," Mom said in a tone that didn't warrant argument. "Let's leave your sister alone for a while." She ushered me out of Quinn's room into the hallway and closed the door behind us.

"Aren't you going to talk to her?" I asked.

Mom looked tired. "I am. But I'm going to give her some time first. I can't make decisions for her."

"But she's making a huge mistake!"

Mom lifted her hand to my cheek. "People make mistakes sweetheart. That's a part of life."

149

"Yeah, yeah whatever."

She smiled at me. "It will be okay. Quinn's a smart girl."

"I guess." I scrunched up my face.

Mom shook her head. "Oh you! What are you doing tonight?"

"Hanging out with you?"

"Sounds great. You pick a movie. I'll go start the popcorn."

"Deal."

Back when Dad had been alive, this was how Mom and I spent our bonding time. These days, though, we didn't do it nearly as often as we used to.

I took the stairs two at a time into the living room. I skimmed through our movie collection, taking longer than usual to make a selection. Something told me a romantic comedy wasn't the best choice for either of our emotions right now, same with drama. Mom hated horror, I hated action. Eventually I ended up picking some lame-looking cartoon/comedy, which didn't turn out to be half as bad as I imagined. I fell asleep during the movie; Mom must have taken me upstairs and put me to bed because that's where I woke up.

14.

I opened my eyes on the day that I had been dreading for a whole year. I really wished I hadn't told Matt I would go snowboarding. Although it had seemed like a good idea at the time, I currently felt like I could spend the whole day buried in a sea of blankets. My heart was heavy. The pain I had carried in my chest for months was swelling so baldly today I thought it was going to break through the skin.

I finally forced myself to get out of bed. The first anniversary of a death is never easy. Not that I knew from experience; today already was harder than all of the days before combined. It's concrete and final, meaning that person is really gone, they've been gone for a while and definitely aren't coming back. It's a constant pang that haunts your heart.

I changed into sweats and a t-shirt to wear under my snow gear and went downstairs to eat. I was not hungry. However I knew that spending the day on the mountain, food was essential. My stomach felt like someone had dropped a massive bulldozer on it.

Quinn was working. I don't know why. It was very typical of Quinn – distracting herself with her career so she could throw herself into something and not have to think. Most people never caught on to this game Quinn played. She had an extreme thirst for perfectionism, but she hid a lot.

The kitchen was empty when I went downstairs. I assumed Robert was already at work. This surprised me; I thought he would have at least taken the day off to be with

Mom. I grabbed two slices of bread from the bag on the counter, popped them into the toaster, peeled myself a banana and walked into the family room. Mom was sitting on the couch staring out the window. I cocked my head to the side to see if there was anything worth staring at. Just the snow falling softly outside.

Mom looked beautiful but broken. She sat on the couch wrapped in a black blanket. Her blonde waves fell lightly around her face. Her green eyes were filled with sadness and brimming with tears. She had dark hollow bags under her eyes and her lips were turned downward into a composed frown. I turned away from her. I could see the pain on her face and it was like a kick in the stomach. Thinking back to all those months where I convinced myself she didn't care about Dad's death, this one image of her immediately hit me with a tidal wave of guilt.

The toaster rang from the kitchen and I jumped. Mom still didn't move. I didn't say anything and walked back into the kitchen. I quickly buttered my toast. The phone rang and I answered it. It was Matt.

"I'm picking Conner up first," he said. "Callie will be at your house in five and I'll swing bye and grab you guys."

"Sounds good. See you soon."

"Bye babe." I hung up the phone and turned around to see Mom standing behind me motionless. I jumped.

"You scared me!" I exclaimed, putting my hand over my chest.

"Sorry Aria." She gave me a small smile, but even that looked painful. "Are you guys leaving soon?" I took a bite of my toast and swallowed.

"Yes." I nodded. "Matt's picking me and Callie up in 10."

"Well, have fun." Mom hugged the blanket around her shoulders tightly.

I hesitated. "Mom, are you sure you're going to be okay alone?"

She waved her hand as if to silence me. "I'll be fine." The doorbell rang.

"It's Callie."

"I'm going upstairs. Have fun today." She started to turn around but I grabbed her by the arm. I wrapped my arms around her in a big hug. She clung to me for a minute and then let go.

"I love you, Mom." I kissed her on the cheek.

"I love you too, sweetheart. Thanks." She bolted up the stairs and I went to go let Callie inside.

I burst out laughing when I saw her. There stood Callie in a pair of white snow pants and possibly the brightest neon pink jacket I had ever seen, along with matching pink gloves and a pink toque. Her jacket had a massive hood lined with light pink fur that tucked around her face. She managed to look cute and completely ridiculous at the same time.

"You know you can put your snow gear on when we get to the mountain right?"

"It's freezing out," she complained. "Besides, I want to go snowboarding when we get to the mountain, not change my wardrobe."

Matt's truck pulled into the driveway. He honked the horn.

I grabbed my duffle bag and shrugged into my blue snow jacket, not nearly as eccentric as Callie's. I closed the front door behind me and joined Callie on the porch.

"Hey – how are you feeling today?" She asked as we walked down the walkway to Matt's truck.

"I'm okay. I don't really want to talk about it. I just want to have fun today."

Callie smiled at me and linked her arm through mine. "That I can do."

We went snowboarding up in The Falls. This was my first time there. It was basically a huge mountain with a resort near Jordan Falls, about an hour drive up the mountain from town. Callie said it was great for hiking in the summer and that there were lots of waterfalls and swimming holes.

The mountain was beautiful, a lot bigger than I expected and covered with fresh snow. Light flakes sprinkled down from the sky.

I hadn't been snowboarding in a long time. Truth be told, I had probably embellished my snowboarding skills to Matt a little more than I should have.

Callie and I started out on the bunny slopes. After I was feeling more confident, Matt and Connor came back for us and we hit up some of the more difficult runs. I held my board in one hand and Matt's gloved hand in the other as we walked toward the chairlift.

Matt and I were silly and flirty on the 15-minute ride to the top. I snuggled into him as close as I could and listened to him talk about Christmas and this new baseball glove his Dad was getting him. I didn't care about the glove, but I loved the sound of his voice. As we approached the top of the mountain I started to get a bit nervous. I wasn't so great with chairlifts.

"Ready?" Matt's voice rang out.

I swallowed. "Yup." The chair came to the small bank of snow where we needed to get off.

"Grab my hands," Matt said, grabbing my gloved fingertips and helping me keep my balance.

"I love you," I said, when we had reached the bottom and I was still standing on both feet.

He smiled and kissed me on the forehead. "You looked nervous."

"I was! I hate the chairlift."

"I figured based on the amount of time you spent on the bunny hills," he teased.

"I'm from the city, okay? We don't have a lot of mountains there!"

He laughed. "Let's go! Race you to the bottom." And off he went with me trailing behind him. He stopped in the middle of the run and waited for me to catch up.

"Lean forward more!" he called as I made my way towards him, "you're leaning back too much." I leaned forward and face planted right in front of his feet. I stood up glaring at him. "I didn't mean that much," he said softly.

"Ha!" I barked and stood up, wiping the snow off myself. "Thanks."

"Watch me." Matt started rocking back and forth on his board. "Do it this way." I watched him go down a little farther. "Now try."

I mimicked his movements and went slowly down the mountain behind him.

"Good! Awesome job, babe!" He kissed me as I reached his side.

"Thanks!" And off we went down the rest of the run, me feeling slightly more adventurous then before.

We were famished around noon, so we went into the lodge cafeteria for lunch. Matt and Connor both got a hamburger and hot dog each, while Callie and I got chicken wraps. We sat down at a picnic table by the fireplace.

"I'm starving!" Connor exclaimed, placing his tray on the table and sitting down. "That was nuts."

"Yeah, the run conditions are awesome today," Callie agreed.

I took a huge bite out of my wrap and nodded in agreement.

"So what are you guys doing for Christmas?" Matt asked, and took a bite of his hot dog.

Callie's whole family grandparents, aunts, uncles and cousins were coming to stay with her. Connor was lying low at home with his parents and brother. Matt's grandparents were flying in from Nova Scotia tomorrow to stay with his family for the holidays. We hadn't really discussed what we were doing as a family. Probably just the whole dinner thing on Christmas day, nothing over the top.

After lunch, we headed back out to the slopes again and messed around on the bunny slopes some more with the guys, mostly just playing and tossing snowballs at each other. It was exactly what I needed to keep my mind occupied.

"I want to try the black diamond," Connor said.

"I don't know man," Matt looked hesitant. "That's one of the toughest runs here."

"What are you chicken, Lawson?" Connor nudged Matt playfully in the ribs. What was with guys and their blatant pride all the time?

"No," Matt said. "I'm not chicken. I was just thinking about the girls." What a sweetheart – or not. I felt slightly irritated by that comment. If he didn't want to go on a run he didn't need to use Callie or me for an excuse, regardless of how either one of us felt about it.

"Whatever," Callie cut in. "We'll be fine, right Aria?" I shot Callie a death glare. I definitely was not ready for one of the hardest runs on the mountain. Callie either didn't pick up on my look or chose to ignore it.

"Let's go then," Connor grinned. He picked up his board and started walking over to a chair lift in the distance. Matt followed him. I felt another flash of irritation.

I turned to Callie. "Are you crazy? I can't go on a black run!"

"You'll be fine," Callie said. "We can just take it slow, okay?" Easy for her to say.

I felt sick the whole ride up the mountain and wasn't at all comforted staring down at the run.

"Relax babe," Matt said. "It's not that bad of a run." He squeezed my hand. I shot him an unimpressed glare and didn't respond. "Don't be mad!" He nuzzled my neck.

"I'm not mad," I said, even though I was. "I just don't want to go on this run. You should have known that."

"Look, I'm sorry." He gave me these sad puppy dog eyes. "When I'm around the guys sometimes I just get a little competitive, that's all. Forgive me?" He flashed me that smile again. How could I not?

I rolled my eyes at him. "Does your charm get you out of everything?"

"It usually doesn't hurt." He grinned again and then leaned in for a kiss that took my breath away.

20 minutes later, we reached the top and my nerves had finally settled.

Callie looked like she was ready to step into a boxing ring. "Ready to show these guys what we're made of?" she asked.

"You're such a goon. Let's go."

Matt and Connor took off down the mountain before us. Callie and I took our time. The steep run had a lot of sharp turns. I was out of breath within the first five minutes.

"Cal!" I called out to her. "Slow down! I'm dying back here."

"Have you not been working out over the holidays?" she grunted.

"What are you girls doing back there?" Matt's voice called from ahead.

"Coming!" I called back, picking up my pace. We finally caught up to the guys.

"The next part's a little rough," Connor warned. More rough than that?

I looked at the steep hill below me and began to slide down it, cringing. I stopped and knelt backwards for a moment. I made my way around the next corner and then it was all a blur.

I turned the corner just in time to see Matt's snowboard flying through the air and off the roped ledge in front of him. I screamed. I heard Connor call out his name. I stopped, ripped the bindings off my board, hopped out of it and ran as fast as I could without falling towards the ledge.

Connor grabbed me and held me back from the ledge. "Aria, wait!" I peered over the rope. Below was what looked like at least a 15-foot deep ravine. Matt was face down in the snow, visible mainly due to his green and black snow jacket.

"Matt!" I screamed hysterically.

"I'm going to go get help," Connor said. "Callie, I need you to stay here with Aria."

"Okay." Callie looked like she was about to burst into tears.

"I need to go down there, Connor." I grabbed onto the marker and tried to maneuver myself around the ledge.

Connor's strong arms grabbed me by the waist and hauled me back and away from the ledge. "Stay here," he ordered. He turned to Callie. "Don't let her move."

"Connor – I don't know if –"

"Callie," he said firmly. "We're wasting time. I'll be back with help." And off he went.

I sat there completely numb. "I need to go get him."

"You can't, Aria," Callie said, shaking her head. "We don't know the conditions down there. The bank could collapse. We don't need two of you hurt."

I peered over the ledge again. "Callie, he's not moving."

She didn't answer, just grabbed my hand and slowly led me back away from the ledge. I started to cry. This couldn't be happening. Not today.

After about 10 minutes – which felt like forever – Connor was back with help. Four first-aid paramedics on snowmobiles plunged down into the ravine and brought Matt back up. He was still unconscious at this point. They air-lifted him to the hospital. I kept telling myself over and over again that I was dreaming.

The drive to the hospital took almost an hour. I cried almost the whole way there, while Callie called our parents to let them know what was happening. I kept repeating the same silent prayer for Matt's well-being in my head. He had to be okay, he just had to be.

I sat between Callie and Connor in the hospital waiting room, trying not to freak out but feeling like I was going insane. I didn't know how Matt was. No one would tell us. I put my head between my legs and took deep long breaths. Callie rubbed my back. Connor was ghostly white.

I had called Mom the second we had arrived at the hospital and she was on her way. I remember last year when Dad died, how we had sat in the waiting room for hours waiting and waiting, and then the doctor had come out and told us he wasn't going to make it. All we knew about Matt was that he was still unconscious. I couldn't help like feeling that this Christmas was going to be a repeat of last year.

"Aria!" My head snapped up. I saw Quinn walking towards me. I ran over to her and fell into her arms.

"Is he okay?" I asked looking up into her green eyes.

"He is," Quinn smiled at me. "He's awake now. He has a concussion and a broken wrist – just a small fracture that should heal up quickly. But he'll be just fine. His parents are with him now."

"Can I see him?" I asked hopefully.

"Yes," Quinn smiled. "You can all see him now."

"Thanks, Quinnie." I quickly hugged her again. "I was so worried that he wasn't going to be –"

"I know," she interrupted. "But he's fine now. Everything's fine. So stop worrying and go see your boyfriend!" She patted me on the head and ushered us towards Matt's room.

Matt was sitting on a bed, still wearing his snow clothes and talking to his dad. Carol was there too. His arm was already in a cast and he was smiling. I immediately threw my arms around him and buried my face in his chest.

"I'm so glad you're okay!"

He patted me on the back. "I'm fine babe. No big deal. Hey, Aria – don't cry."

I was confused at first and then felt the tears rolling down my cheeks. I felt silly. "Sorry," I said blushing. I stood up.

"Don't be sorry, Aria," Peter said. His deep voice was soft and reassuring. "Matt gave us all a bit of a scare."

"That he did," Carol agreed. "Did you know our Matt has had five concussions already?"

"Is that true?" I asked him.

He nodded and a smile crossed his lips. "Lots of baseballs in the head growing up."

Mom burst through the door to Matt's room, looking frantic. "Is everything okay?"

"Just a concussion, and this," Matt held up his wrist, "which totally sucks." Mom walked over to Matt and gave him a hug, which surprised me.

"Well I'm glad you're okay," she told him. "Aria told me you had everyone quite worried."

"Yeah, I was out for a while." Matt shook his head. "Doc said I need to wear a helmet from now on. I can't afford another concussion."

"You all should have been wearing helmets," Mom scolded.

"They don't make helmets that go with my snowsuit," Callie said, completely sincere. Mom stared at her for a moment, trying to decide if she was serious or not, then just gave her a strange nod and walked towards the door.

"Come on, slugger," Peter said, putting his hand on Matt's shoulder. "Let's get you home."

Matt stood up and came over to me. "Can you come over later?"

"After you rest!" Carol called to him.

"After I rest," Matt mimicked.

"I'm having dinner with Mom and Quinn," I told him, "but I'll call you after and see how you're feeling, okay?"

"Sure," Matt said. "Are we still meeting tomorrow to exchange Christmas presents?"

"You bet." I rested my arms lightly on his shoulders and kissed him firmly on the lips. "Love you."

"Love you too, baby."

"Let's get a move on it, lovebirds!" Peter chuckled.

"Funny," Matt stuck out his tongue at his father.

"I thought it was," Peter grinned.

I walked over to where Mom was standing with Carol and linked my arm through hers. "Let's go!"

Mom drove me home from the hospital. We were quiet most of the way home. "Thanks for coming," I said quietly.

"You're welcome, sweetheart." Mom's eyes didn't shift away from the road. "I'm just glad Matt's okay."

"So am I." I smiled at her.

"So what are we going to make for dinner?" Mom asked. Her voice brightened a little.

"Is Robert going to be home?"

"I'm not sure," Mom said. "He told me that if I wanted him there he would be, but thought it might be nice for the three of us girls to do something together."

"Quinn said she'll be home soon."

"Why don't we order Chinese for dinner?" Chinese was Dad's top favourite food. Back home in Toronto, we all would go to this place called the Golden Dragon every Friday night.

"I think that would be great." Mom pulled into our driveway that was once again covered with a thick layer of snow. "Do you know how long this is supposed to keep up?" I gestured outside.

"It's supposed to warm up in a week or so."

"Ah." I got out of the car. It was starting to get dark outside already. I glanced at my watch and was surprised that it was almost 5 o'clock. "Does the Chinese place deliver?" I walked up the walkway to the front door.

"I think so. When did Quinn say she would be home?"

"She's off at five."

"I'll place the order now then. The usual?"

I smiled at this question. When Dad was alive, we had always gotten the same order for as long as I could remember. "The usual sounds great, Mom." I let myself in the house and went upstairs to get changed for dinner.

Quinn walked in the front door just as the food had arrived. "Oh good, I'm starving." She dropped her bag on the ground and sat down at the table. "Chinese." Quinn stared at the food on the table and didn't say anything more.

Mom joined us at the table. She too stared at the food. I couldn't for the life of me remember the last time we had had Chinese food. I looked at the wonton soup, one of Dad's favourite dishes. I didn't know what else to do, I began to spoon some into my bowl, then Quinn's, then Mom's.

Mom put her hand on mine. "Thanks, sweetie."

"You're welcome." I took a sip of my soup. I could feel the sadness at the dinner table. It was like a heavy rainfall was pouring down over the three of us, completely drenching us from head to toe.

"This sucks." Quinn finally spoke up. It was unlike Quinn to admit to defeat. I didn't know what to say. We both turned to look at Mom, waiting for something.

To my disbelief, Mom started laughing. Her laughter rang throughout the entire kitchen. It was loud and on the verge of hysteria. My mouth dropped open and I watched her. I looked at Quinn who shrugged and then began to stir her soup counter clockwise.

"Mom?" I stared at her, my face filled with concern. "What's so funny?" Mom now had tears of laughter rolling down her cheeks. She wiped them away.

"Oh nothing," she laughed even harder. "This just does really suck." I didn't know what to say. I slowly nodded my head in agreement. I looked at Quinn again who to my dismay began to laugh as well. It was official, I was living with crazy people. I continued to stare at the two of them as though they had both gone completely bonkers.

And then something strange happened. I began to laugh. Mostly because I didn't know what else to do. I started to laugh like I hadn't laughed in years. First softly and then a complete out roar of hysterical laughter. The three of us sat there laughing until we were all crying and doubled over with stomach pain. It was wonderfully awful, one of those moments of irony that just slips past you. When the laughter had stopped and we dug into the chicken chow mein, it was finally Quinn who broke the long silence.

"I miss his laugh," she said. I thought of Dad's laugh. Loud and booming. You could be blindfolded in a room, but hear that laugh and know it was his.

"I miss his hugs," Mom said. "And his smile." I thought for a moment. There were so many things about Dad that I missed. I didn't even know where to start.

"I miss how he always believed in me and challenged me to always go after my heart," I said. I gave them both the tiniest smile I could muster without completely breaking down. Mom took my hand in her left and Quinn's in her right.

"Your father would be so proud of you both." She smiled at us, her eyes wet with tears. "He loved you very much and more than anything wanted you to be happy."

Now I gave her a real smile.

"I can't believe it's been a whole year," Quinn said, looking shocked.

I shook my head. "I know. It went by so quickly."

"It will get easier, my babies," Mom squeezed my hand. "I promise."

We didn't talk about Dad for the rest of the night after that. In some ways, this was relieving. After dinner we went into the living room and visited. It had been a while since we had hung out together, just the three of us. I was comforted having Mom and Quinn beside me, knowing they probably felt the same way right now.

Later that night I went upstairs to my room to call Matt. I was actually happy. The hollow feeling in my stomach from earlier in the day had passed. I dialed his number. He answered on the first ring.

"You're alive," he said.

"Sorry," I laughed. "I was with Mom and Quinn all night. How are you feeling?"

"Don't be sorry," he said softly. "Family is important. You needed to be with yours today. I'm feeling fine."

"Fine?"

"Mom won't leave my side," he said in an annoyed tone. "She keeps waking me up every hour."

"I'm pretty sure that's mandatory."

"I feel great," he insisted.

"Oh yeah? Great enough to snowboard down a mountain again?"

"Maybe not that great," he laughed. "Okay, so my wrist is a little sore. But as soon as school starts up again, I'm going to need to hit the gym hard. Can't let a little injury hold me back. Doc said I should only have this cast on for a month."

"When does baseball start?" I asked.

"We start training in January and hit the field as soon as the snow is gone. Usually March."

"That seems early."

"It is, but we need to be the best. Basketball playoffs start next week, right?"

"Yup." I frowned, even though he couldn't see it. I hadn't thought twice about basketball since school started. "I haven't practiced much."

"Kind of hard with all the snow."

"Callie wants to have a practice at the school after Christmas."

"Callie's crazy," Matt confirmed. "Enjoy your vacation."

"I don't think the word 'vacation' is in Callie's vocabulary," I laughed. "So what time do you want me to come over tomorrow?"

"I want you to come over right now," Matt said.

"Hm…how about first thing tomorrow?" I smiled.

"How about now?" I could picture his grin.

"Mom won't let me drive in this snow. The roads should be plowed in the morning."

"Okay, I'll take it," Matt said. "Do you want to come over for breakfast? I can cook."

"With one hand?"

"Do you doubt my cooking skills?"

"Never." I smiled again. My heart felt like it was pounding out of my chest with happiness. I'd never had this feeling before.

"Good. Come over around 10?"

"Perfect." I sighed and sank back into the pillows on my bed.

"Don't forget my present," he teased.

"Present?" I joked. "You mean I was supposed to get you something?" He laughed. I had bought him an expensive sports watch that he had been eyeing since Thanksgiving, as well as a new baseball bag I knew he wanted. I had no idea what he had gotten me, though he had been teasing me about it for weeks.

"Okay, Mom's back with my medicine, so I have to go."

"Tell her I say hello." He did.

"She says hi back. I love you."

"I love you more."

"Impossible. Good night, babe."

"Sweet dreams." I hung up the phone.

You know that feeling that you get when you are about to get on a roller coaster? You're terrified and yet there's something so thrilling about the experience that makes you want to get on and do it again. Even though the hills are scary, that feeling of soaring through the air is so amazing. That's how Matt made me feel. He was my rollercoaster. I couldn't imagine my life without him and I didn't know how I had ever lived before I found him.

I slept well that night. I was at peace. Life was good. I was actually looking forward to Christmas now.

15.

I woke up the next morning and looked out the window. The snow had stopped. I ran downstairs. Robert was sitting at the kitchen table reading the paper with a coffee mug plastered to his hand.

"Good morning," he glanced up at me.

"Hey," I said. "Where's Mom?"

"Sleeping."

"It's 9 o'clock!"

"I don't think she slept well last night," Robert's eyes were filled with sympathy.

"Can I drive over to Matt's?"

"Should be fine," he said. "I was out this morning and the main roads are clear. You can take the truck." He tossed me his keys. "Be home by four for dinner? Your mother wants us to all go to church tonight."

"Okay. Thanks."

"How is Matt feeling?" he asked. I walked over to the counter and poured myself some coffee.

"His wrist is a little sore." I took a sip of the coffee. "This is really good. New kind?"

"It's bolder," he replied. "Well I'm glad he's okay."

"Me too."

Robert closed his paper. "What are you guys doing today?"

"Exchanging Christmas presents," I grinned.

"Oooo," Robert whistled. "Have fun with that."

"Thanks. Okay I'm going to go get ready. Tell Mom I'm at Matt's?"

"Will do." He stood up to refill his coffee and I went upstairs to change.

Within 10 minutes I was out the door and on my way to Matt's house. The roads were a little icy but nothing Robert's truck couldn't handle. I parked in the driveway and bolted to the front door, carrying a bag with Matt's Christmas presents by my side.

Rachel opened the door and let me in. "Hey Aria," she hugged me. "Merry Christmas."

"Merry Christmas," I smiled at her.

"Matt's upstairs in his room. You can go on up." I hesitated for a second. I had never been in Matt's room before. In his house we always hung out downstairs. She must have caught on. "Second door on the left."

I nodded. "Thanks." I walked up the huge spiral staircase in the Lawson's foyer. When I reached his door I knocked.

"Come in," he called. I pushed the door open slowly and poked my head inside.

Matt's room was your typical boy's room. Not that I made a habit of being in boy's rooms. Dark blue walls were splashed with posters and flyers of baseball teams and players. One wall was lined with ribbons, trophies and awards. A desk with a neat stack of books piled on top was in one corner and a bag full of sports equipment in the other.

Matt was lying on a blue and gray stripped comforter on his bed. He had an ice pack on his arm right above his cast. The TV was on and he was watching baseball, of course.

"Welcome to my pad," he said.

"Your pad?" I repeated in a mocking tone.

"Mmhmm. What do you think?"

I looked around the room again. "It's very you."

"Well that's too bad. I was trying to go for you."

"Very funny." I walked over to the shelf lined with trophies and awards and began reading. Most Valuable Player, Most Sportsman-Like, Most Aggressive (this one surprised me)...the list went on. "You're a pretty big deal in baseball, hey?"

"And other things," Matt grinned. I shook my head at him. "So are you going to stand there and look at my trophies all day or come and give me a kiss?" I grinned and crossed the room. I sat down on his bed and kissed him.

"All better?" I asked.

"Much," he slid his arm around me. "So do you want to open your present now? Or breakfast?"

"Why are you even asking me that?" I frowned.

"Right!" Matt hopped up off the bed. "Breakfast it is. To the kitchen we go!" He ran out of the room.

"Hey that's not what I meant!" I hollered after him. I jumped off the bed and followed Matt downstairs into the kitchen.

"I'm not ready to give you your present quite yet," he told me as we walked into the kitchen. The kitchen was empty, which surprised me. With a family as big as Matt's, people were usually everywhere.

"Where is everyone?" I asked.

"They went into Vancouver. They're picking the grandparents up from the airport and they took all the kids with them. So it's just me and Rach today. Well, and you." How convenient.

"Cool," I replied.

"Very." Matt opened the fridge door and looked around. "So how about an omelet? My specialty."

"An omelet would be great." I pursed my lips together.

"Any preferences?" Matt started pulling eggs, milk and other food out of the fridge.

"Surprise me."

"Done." He closed the fridge door. "Hey Rachel!" He yelled.

Rachel appeared in the kitchen seconds later. "What's up?"

"What are you doing?"

"Reading," she held up a large leather-bound novel.

"Do you want some breakfast?" Matt held up the carton of eggs.

"That would be awesome," Rachel said. "Do you need any help?"

Matt glanced around the kitchen. "I think we've got it covered. Although I'm not sure about Aria's cooking skills."

"Hey!" I protested.

Rachel laughed. "I see Matt's being charming as always."

"He usually is charming!" I pointed out.

"True," she agreed. "For a little brother there are definitely worse options out there."

"Thanks," Matt rolled his eyes. "I'll call you when yours is ready."

"Excellent." Rachel shot him a smile and walked out of the kitchen.

"So what you do want me to do?" I asked.

"Ever cracked an egg before?" Matt sounded completely serious, which made me chuckle.

I raised my eyebrows at him. "I'm from the city. We do have eggs there."

"Okay, okay." Matt held up his hands in surrender. "Knock yourself out." I took one egg and smacked it on the side of the glass bowl he placed in front of me. Matt grimaced.

"What?" I asked, holding back my eye roll.

"Nothing," he said. He put some mushrooms on a cutting board and began chopping. "Well it's just…here, do it like this." He grabbed two eggs and showed me how to crack them against one another. I followed his action.

"Why does it matter that I'm doing it this way?"

"Beats me," Matt shrugged. "I saw it on the cooking network once. Plus it makes you look really cool." I laughed and continued cracking the eggs the way he showed me.

After I had cracked all the eggs, Matt let me whisk and season them. I made us some coffee and set the table while he cooked. Soon enough the aroma of coffee, butter and bacon filled the kitchen.

Rachel wandered in and sat down at the table with me. "This smells great, Mattie," she remarked.

"It really does," I added.

Matt took a small bow and walked over to the table with a plate of omelets. He served one for me and one for Rachel.

"Dig in, ladies!" He dropped down into his chair and cut into his own omelet.

The taste of cheese, meat, mushrooms, tomato and spinach filled my mouth. "You were right," I turned to Matt after I had swallowed. "This is the best omelet ever."

Rachel nodded. "You've got a keeper with this one, Aria. When we were growing up Matt was addicted to watching the Food Network. He would even try to fake sick to stay home from school and watch cooking shows! Mom used him a lot to help her cook. When we were really little, he would even steal my Easy Bake Oven!"

"Shhh!" Matt elbowed her. "You aren't supposed to tell people that. It makes me look less cool."

"I think you'll be okay," I told him. "So when did baseball take over your cooking passion? Why not be a chef?"

Matt stroked his chin as if he was thinking long and hard about this question. "If I were a chef, I'd want my own restaurant on my own terms. I don't think I have it in me for that. Cooking is fun for me; I wouldn't want it to become work. It's how I unwind."

"Interesting."

"Very," he echoed. I took another bite of my omelet.

"What are you guys doing today?" Rachel asked.

"Robbing a bank," Matt replied with a straight face. I shook my head and laughed.

"Have fun with that one, buddy. You're on your own."

"Can you ever be serious?" Rachel asked him.

"No way," Matt grinned and polished off the rest of his omelet.

"I think we're just hanging out here," I told Rachel. "Matt needs to rest. How is your arm by the way?"

"Better now that you're here," he grabbed both my hands and gazed into my eyes. I swatted him away.

"You are such a cornball!"

"Agreed." Rachel stood up and took her plate over to the dishwasher. "Well, thanks for breakfast you guys. I'll see you later."

"Alone at last," Matt commented, once she had left the room.

"Hush," I told him. "She's your sister."

"And?" He stretched his good arm out behind my chair.

"Be nice." I began to clear the plates off the table. "Let's get this place cleaned up."

We cleaned the kitchen together. I cleaned, rinsed and dried the dishes and Matt put them away with his one arm. I got him another ice pack for his arm and we collapsed on an oversized couch in the living room. I rested my head on his shoulder and listened to his soft breathing.

I tilted my head back and looked up into his eyes. "Can I give you your present now?"

"Of course," he grinned. "I'll go get yours." He returned a few minutes later with a big box.

"Here, open mine first." I handed him the two boxes.

He opened the big box with the baseball bag in it first. I watched as his face broke out into a massive smile.

"Aria! I can't believe you! This is awesome." He examined the side of the bag where I had gotten his name and jersey number embroidered. "You're amazing."

"Open the next one," I gestured towards the smaller box. He did.

"You spoil me way too much," he shook his head at me. He fastened the watch around his wrist. "I've had my eye on this for a while. Thank you baby."

"You're welcome." I leaned in for a kiss. I opened my eyes and he handed me a small black jewelry box. My heart skipped a beat wondering what was inside.

"Open it," Matt breathed. I did. I almost fell to the floor, unsure of how to react when I saw what was inside. A ring. A beautiful, white gold ring with a small heart diamond in the centre. I was at a loss for words. "It's a promise ring," Matt clarified. I sunk back into a calm state. "I know we haven't been dating that long, Aria, but I am completely intoxicated by you. I want to spend the rest of my life with you – when we are old enough of course, but that's why I wanted to get you this. To symbolize forever."

I felt my knees go weak for a moment. He put the ring on my right ring finger. "Do you like it?" Matt asked. I realized I hadn't spoken yet.

I wet my lips. "It's beautiful." I wrapped my arms around his neck. "I don't even know what to say Matt. This is the best present ever. You are so wonderful."

"I'm so in love with you," he whispered the words softly into my ear.

"The feeling is mutual," I responded. I closed my eyes and tried to imagine the last time when everything in my life had felt so perfect. I couldn't. We stood there quietly in each other's arms for what felt like hours. We enjoyed the silence of the house and the complete bliss of being lost in one another.

16.

That night we had our usual Christmas Eve traditions. Mom made a bunch of appetizers and we all hung around eating food and chatting with one another. I, however, was on cloud nine. A small part of me almost felt guilty for being so happy. I knew Mom and Quinn were both having a rough time remembering Dad. I couldn't help it though and I knew if Dad were still alive, he would want me to be happy. So I was.

Church that night started at 7 o'clock. I was much more calm about going this time. I pranced towards the car with Robert and heard Quinn say to Mom, "What's with Happy?"

"She's in love," Mom softly told Quinn, to which Quinn replied with some sarcastic remark about how love wasn't everything. I knew she was hurting, so I didn't take it personally.

The church parking lot was jam-packed. We found seats together closer to the back of the church. I saw Matt who was sitting up front with his family. He winked at me and I melted. I sighed and sank down into the pew.

"She's got it bad," Quinn observed dryly. I just smiled at her.

The service was short. Not that I would have minded tonight. We sang some Christmas carols and the pastor briefly told the Christmas story. We went home shortly after. When we got home Mom took us all into the family room. She lit a candle and turned off all the lights except for the Christmas tree. The tree shone brightly in the dark room, as did the candle.

The four of us sat on the couch together. "This candle is for your father," she told us all.

I thought about this for a moment. I thought about Dad. I felt at peace about it. I still felt a layer of sadness that was spread over my heart, but I knew I was going to be okay. I looked at Mom. She was smiling. She had tears in her eyes, but a smile on her face. She took the candle and placed it in front of the window. There it shone brightly, for al the world to see.

17.

The rest of Christmas vacation flew by. I spent most of it with Matt and family. Finally came the Monday morning in January where it was time to return to school. I was dreading my last semester of high school. For starters, college applications were due in two weeks and I hadn't yet applied anywhere. Mom nagged me about it every chance she got. My course load this semester consisted of calculus, physics, English literature and a spare. I wasn't sure how I was going to handle calculus and physics.

Matt picked me up on the first morning back to school, as usual. The snow had subsided right after New Years and it was now pouring rain outside. Matt's arm was still casted. He had an appointment scheduled with the doctor the following week to remove the cast and have his arm x-rayed. The doctor told him he needed to do a bunch of strengthening exercises every day in order to strengthen his arm for baseball season.

Matt's semester was a lot less intense than mine. Fitness, a spare, English and cafeteria. Definitely a slack semester, but one that was easy for him during baseball season.

"Ready to go back?" Matt asked as we drove to school.

I watched the rain fall out the passenger window. "Not even a little bit. I'm really worried about my course load. I still have a month of basketball season left – maybe even longer."

"You will be fine," Matt reassured me. "Do you have practice today?"

"Yeah."

"Want me to wait around and drive you home after? I think I'm going to do some extra training after school anyways."

"If you want. You don't have to though."

"I offered."

"Okay," I smiled. "That would be great."

We pulled up to the school and I got out of his truck. He took my hand and walked me to my locker. The first bell rang.

"Where's your first class?" he asked.

"Upstairs. Calc."

"I've got to get to the gym. I'll see you at lunch?"

"If I'm still alive by then," I cringed.

"Relax babe," he kissed me on the cheek. "I'll see you later."

"Bye." I walked down the hall to where Callie was buried in her locker. We had calculus and physics together, which was the only good thing about my course load.

"How's it going?" I greeted her.

"Meh. I had to meet with Mr. Bowman this morning." Mr. Bowman was our school guidance counsellor. "He thinks I need to apply to a few more safety schools. This means I am going to spend tonight filling out even more applications."

"How many schools have you applied to?"

"Five."

I immediately felt panic wash over me. "Beats my zero."

"You haven't applied anywhere?" Callie shot me a look of disapproval. She closed her locker and we began to walk down the hallway together.

"I have no idea what I want to do," I moaned.

"Aria! You don't have much time!"

"You sound like my mother."

"Well maybe she has a point," Callie shot back.

"I don't even know if I want to go to school right away."

"Where has Matt applied?" She raised her eyebrows at me.

"I don't know," I muttered. "All schools in the States I think."

"None in Canada?"

"Nope," I tried not to let my face sink. "He doesn't want to stay here. He will probably get a baseball scholarship. He wants to go to Florida."

"Why don't you apply there?"

I laughed. "Well, first off, my grades aren't good enough."

"Your grades aren't that bad, Aria." We reached our class and found seats towards the back of the room.

"They aren't good enough and I don't think my mom can afford to send me to a school out there."

"So are you not applying to schools because you don't want to be away from Matt?"

"That's stupid," I pointed out.

"Exactly."

"I guess," I said uncertainly. I really didn't want to think about the future. I wanted to stay in this year of my life where everything was perfect for as long as possible. "I just don't want things to change."

"Change is a part of life," Callie said sternly.

I rolled my eyes. "Thanks, Cal." The second bell rang which signaled that it was time for class to begin.

I spent the next hour feeling completely frantic, especially because calculus was a foreign language to me. I had no clue why I was taking these stupid classes. Well, I did – because Mom expected me to. But it's not like I wanted to be a doctor or anything. I remember starting high school and both my parents sitting me down, telling me I needed to keep my options open for college. This meant taking as many upper-level classes as possible.

I left calculus with a splitting headache and a giant stress ball in the middle of my forehead. Physics wasn't much better. I couldn't wait for lunch time so I could be with Matt. Probably a bad sign if I was already feeling this overwhelmed by the first half of the first day of the semester.

"I'm sure it will get easier," Callie told me as we walked to the cafeteria together.

"You think?" I was skeptical. I was sure it would only get harder.

"Well for starters, I think we'll get used to the work load," Callie shrugged.

"Yeah, 50 practice questions a night! I don't think I'll get used to that anytime soon." That was our homework load for the first day of school. Clearly none of our teachers were holding on to the Christmas spirit.

"I also think they're just trying to scare us," Callie suggested. "You know, last semester of high school. A lot of kids think they can just blow it off."

I shook my head in disgust. "Well that would be nice. When are we even supposed to do all this homework? We have basketball practice after school today."

"We can try to get out early."

"It's our first practice back, Callie. If anything, you know you'll make us stay later."

"Okay fine." Callie pushed her dark hair out of her eyes. "Well we can study together after?"

"That works."

We entered the cafeteria and I scanned the tables looking for Matt. I saw him with a few guys at a table. I squinted to get a better look. One of the guys was Logan. I did a double take. What was Matt doing with him?

"Hey Cal –".

"I thought they didn't talk anymore." Callie said before I could even finish.

"Is Logan on the baseball team?" I asked. I watched Matt who looked like he was actually being friendly with Logan.

Callie looked flustered. "He used to be. I don't know what Matt thinks he's doing. Logan is trouble. Big trouble."

"So I keep hearing." My head began to pound even more. "I need coffee."

Callie sighed. "Sounds better than this."

I linked my arm through hers and steered her out of the cafeteria. I searched for a vending machine and inserted a dollar when I found one. I hit the button for the most caffeinated beverage I could find and drank it in about four swigs. Callie bought one for herself.

I went back into the cafeteria with a reluctant, fussy Callie. Matt was now sitting with Connor and Logan was nowhere to be seen.

"See? He's gone," I said to Callie.

"I don't want to see Connor either," she sighed.

"Why?"

"Because," she said, "he likes me and I don't want to deal with that. I'm going to the library. I'll see you at practice, okay?" I walked over to Matt and sat down beside him.

"Hey," I said.

"Hey yourself," he kissed me. "Where have you been?"

"Headache," I explained. "I needed caffeine."

"Got it."

"How's your arm feeling?"

"It's sore," Matt held out his casted arm and rotated it in a circular motion. "I did a lot of exercise this morning though."

"Be careful," I warned him. "You don't want to hurt yourself even more."

"I'll be fine," he reassured me.

"So how was your morning besides that?" I asked.

"Easy," he smiled.

"Our classes are murder," I whined. "My brain felt like it was going to explode all morning."

"I'm sure it will get easier."

I didn't want to beat around the bush anymore. Besides, I knew Callie would ask me the second I saw her. "So why were you talking to Logan?"

"Oh," Matt said. "He was just giving me some rehab tips for my arm."

"The kind that will land you in a different kind of rehab centre," Connor remarked.

"What?" Matt looked confused.

189

"Everyone knows Logan's into drugs," Connor said with disgust.

"Everyone?" Matt now looked irritated. "Pretty sure he takes a urine sample at the beginning of the season along with the rest of us."

"Maybe he can screen it."

"Whatever," Matt said. "Logan's not that bad and he's not like that."

"He's a total creep," Connor pushed.

"Just drop it okay?" Matt shrugged his shoulders forward. I put my hand over top of his hand in what I hoped was a comforting gesture.

"Whatever, man. Your funeral." A sullen looking Connor looked out the window. Matt was looking the opposite direction across the cafeteria. Callie appeared at my side.

"I thought you were going to the library?" I said, confused.

"Someone else was there," Callie clenched her jaw.

"Logan goes to the library now?"

"Apparently." She sat down on the other side of me. Callie didn't seem bothered by the lull in communication between Matt and Connor; in fact, she didn't appear to notice at all. She said her parents were going out of town this weekend and wanted to have some people over.

"Your parents are letting you have a party?" I was skeptical.

"A few people over," she clarified.

"So a party." It was high school and word got around pretty fast in a town like Jordan Falls.

"I guess," Callie said sheepishly. Her eyes wandered over to Matt. "What's your issue?"

"Nothing," he grumbled.

"Yeah, okay." She looked slightly annoyed. "I'm going to get more fries." She stood up and Connor stood up too.

"I'm going with you," he said. Callie rolled her eyes at me.

When they were more than an earshot away, I turned to face a pouty looking Matt.

"What's wrong, babe?"

"My arm hurts," he said harshly. I was immediately taken back by his tone. The whole time I had known Matt, I don't think I ever saw him angry.

"Sorry." I shrugged my shoulders at him, but my tone was unsympathetic.

"Not your fault," he grumbled.

"I don't like to see you hurting."

"Connor just really pisses me off sometimes," he exploded. I didn't know how he wanted me to response. He looked fuming mad; I didn't know how to deal with this.

"He just doesn't want you to get into any trouble."

"He's a judgmental prick." There was that tone again. I stared at him, not really sure who this guy was that was sitting in front of me.

"A little harsh, don't you think?" I scowled at him.

"Whatever." Matt stood up and slung his backpack over his good arm.

"Where are you going?" I sighed, feeling the worry spread over my face.

"To the library," he said. "I just need to go clear my head for a while, okay?"

I didn't respond, just watched him walk out of the cafeteria and felt as though I could cry. Callie came back over and sat down beside me.

"What's up?" she said, her eyes filled with concern.

"Ask Matt," I sighed. "I don't know what his issue is."

"He's probably just frustrated. The guys are all starting their training for the season, and Matt's injury is going to put him behind."

"He just seems so angry."

"He'll get over it."

"I've never seen him like that before."

"Even Prince Charming has his off days," Callie said lightly. "Anyways, Connor is going to go apologize. They can both be really stubborn sometimes." The bell rang. "What class do you have next?"

"Lit. At least I'll be able to understand that."

"Spare last block?"

"Yup. You?"

"Yeah. Want to start our calc homework?"

"Library?"

"See you then." Callie sauntered out of the cafeteria.

I grabbed my backpack and headed off in the other direction. I spent the rest of the afternoon trying to avoid thinking about Matt. Of course, I silently kicked myself every time his name entered my mind. We had never fought before. Even though I wasn't really sure if what had happened at lunch was a fight, it still didn't feel normal.

In lit class we started reading *Beowulf*. My mind drifted somewhere between the first 10 pages; by the end of class, I was completely lost. I added another packet of discussion questions to my homework pile. When class ended, Matt wasn't waiting outside the door for me. My shoulders felt heavy as I walked towards the library to meet Callie, secretly sneaking glances around me in hopes that I would see him.

Matt wasn't in the library, even though his spare was the same block as ours, and he didn't show up at the gym to watch us play basketball after school. Connor showed up towards the end with a few of the guys and I jogged over to them asking if they'd seen Matt. They told me I would find Matt in the weight room. I slipped out of practice to the weight room but Matt was nowhere to be seen.

I started to panic when he still didn't show up at the end of practice. "I wonder why he's so mad at me," I pouted to Callie. I stood in the locker room showers, letting the hot water pound against my tense, aching muscles.

"He's not mad at you," Callie said. "He's probably just cooling off. Matt doesn't get angry very often. When he does, he usually just needs some space."

"Space?" I turned off the water and wrapped my towel around my body.

"I've known Matt for a long time," she pointed out. "Trust me, it will be fine. Call him when you get home. I'm sure it's just a misunderstanding."

But I didn't want to call him. Now *I* was getting angry. I hadn't done anything wrong and I didn't understand why my boyfriend was being the biggest jerk. So what if he was injured? It still didn't give him the right to blow me off. Callie was sympathetic and let me vent the whole walk home from school.

"Call me later," Callie said as we parted into our separate driveways. I waved and headed into the house. I went straight for the dining room table. It was large and I needed the space to study. I pulled out my physics textbook and began my homework.

I spent the next hour completely enthralled in my studies. I felt like I was finally starting to get the main concept of what we had learned in class. I told myself that I didn't deserve a medal or anything since it was only the first day of class. I was so focused on my homework I didn't even hear Quinn and Mom come into the room.

"Earth to Aria!"

I snapped my head up from my textbook. Quinn stood in front of me, shaking her head.

"What?" I scowled at her.

"Whoa," she held up her hands. "Just came to say hi. What's your issue?"

"Nothing." I looked back down at the book.

"Physics?" Quinn peered over at my textbook. "Need any help?"

"I'm fine."

"Clearly." Her sarcastic tone only irritated me more.

"Sweetheart," Mom said. "Matt called for you."

"Who cares," I said bitterly.

"Sorry?" Quinn was taken back. "Am I hearing this right?"

I sighed. "Sorry. I'm just having the worst day ever."

"Want to talk about it?" Mom asked.

"No," I said firmly. "I just want to finish my million homework questions and go to bed." I watched Mom's eyes carefully study my body language and face. This irritated me even more.

"Dinner will be ready in 20 minutes," she said. "Quinn, come help me. Let your sister study."

I locked my eyes downwards on my textbook once more. I was interrupted minutes later by Robert coming in the front door.

"It's cold out," he called. I could hear him hanging up his coat in the hall closet.

"Whatever," I replied. He came into the same room.

"I think you have a visitor," he motioned towards the front door.

"Who?" I took my hair in my hands and tied it up on top of my head.

"Go see," Robert smiled at me. I rolled my eyes immediately in response. I wasn't in the mood to "go see." I reluctantly stood up from the table and walked towards the front door. "Put a coat on!" he hollered after me.

I shrugged into my ski jacket and boots and went outside onto the front porch. I stood face-to-face with a blue-eyed, glistening, smiling Matt staring at me.

"I'm going back inside," I grumbled and started to turn around. He grabbed my arm.

"Aria, wait."

"What?"

"I'm sorry," he said. "I was a jerk today. In fact, I was more than a jerk. I'm just really stressed about my arm and getting in shape for the season. Logan was trying to help me with my rehab – that's why we were talking today. He had a similar injury a few years back and then Connor just set me off. I really shouldn't have taken it out on you. I'm really sorry." He pulled out a large bouquet of orange and yellow daises from behind his back. "Forgive me?" His eyes twinkled.

"Do you think you can just give me flowers and make everything better?" But even as I said the words, I knew that he could. He had already won my heart.

"No," he admitted. "But it helps."

"It does, does it?"

"Doesn't it?" He grinned.

"Maybe."

He pulled me close with his free arm and kissed me. "I've wanted to do that all day."

I sighed and sank into his arms. "I hate fighting with you," I said. He held me even tighter.

"It does get old," he agreed.

"You need to talk to me when you get upset about something. You can't just run away."

He kissed my forehead. "I promise I will."

"Good." I rested my head on his chest. "Do you want to stay for dinner?"

"Yes, but then I'll leave you alone so you can study."

"Thanks," I stuck my tongue out at him. "Just what I want." I linked my arm through his and pulled him inside the house.

I ran ahead of him into the kitchen. "Can Matt stay for dinner?" I asked Mom.

"Sure," she said.

"All is well in paradise?" Quinn raised her eyebrows and nodded towards the flowers I was holding.

"Yup," I smiled.

"Well that's good."

"It is."

Matt walked into the room and stood behind me. He put his arms around me like he owned me. Not in a possessive, psychopath sort of way, but in a loving you-are-mine-and-only-mine manner. I remember in that moment feeling like nothing could ever come between us. Call me crazy, young and naïve, but a part of me knew that Matt was mine – and I was his – and nothing was ever going to change that.

Matt ate dinner with Robert, Mom, Quinn and me; everything was wonderfully in sync. After dinner, Matt was true to his word and kissed me good night at the door. I went back to a world full of atoms and molecules but found myself daydreaming and having difficulty focusing on homework. Callie called me shortly after and rambled on about the things we needed to do before the weekend to get her house ready for the party. I of course volunteered to be on house patrol with her as any good friend would do.

18.

Callie's parents left for their weekend early Friday morning. After school that day, Matt had a doctor's appointment, so Connor chauffeured Callie and I around town in his old beat up car so we could pick up party favors. When we had enough chips, dip and candy to feed an army, we went back to Callie's house.

I had told Mom and Robert that Callie's parents were away for the weekend and we were having a girl's night. Well, I left a scribbled note on the kitchen counter, knowing that Mom would have never bought my sad excuse of a lie. We then hid valuables, set up bowls of food and began to play around with the music selection.

The girls from the basketball team and some of Matt's friends showed up promptly around 6 o'clock, but Matt was nowhere to be seen. I went into the kitchen and tried him on his cell. I got his voicemail. When I went back into the living room I found it filled with at least double the people that had been there before. More were coming in through the front door.

"Callie, who are all these people?" I asked.

"I have no clue," she called back. "Connor?"

Connor shrugged. "Don't look at me; I didn't invite any of them." I looked around Callie's downstairs level, which was now crawling with teenagers.

"We need to get them out of here," Callie looked like her eyes were going to pop of her head. "My parents are going to kill me." I nodded in agreement.

I turned to my right and saw a tall guy I had never seen before drop a keg on the floor. My eyes widened. "Hey, Callie – " But Callie was already on her way over to this guy telling him he needed to leave. I watched as he responded by inserting the tap into the keg and pouring himself a drink. This was going to be a long night.

An hour later, Matt showed up. He was by Logan's side, an image that I was not entirely comfortable with. I tried to remind myself what Matt had said about Logan, that he was a good guy, just misunderstood. I just couldn't help shake the feeling I had about him. Matt came over to me and planted a long kiss on my lips. I pulled away and got a small taste of something bitter. Beer?

"Have you been drinking?" I asked, stepping backwards.

"Hello to you too," he replied. Great time to cop an attitude.

"You taste like beer."

Matt put his hands in his pockets. "I had a drink on the way over. So what."

"I thought you didn't drink."

"I had one drink, Aria, lighten up. Lots of kids our age drink. It's not a big deal."

"Fine." I turned away from him and stalked off to find Callie. He followed me.

"Don't be like that."

"Be like what?"

"Cold," he said quickly. Too quickly. My eyes burned with tears like I had been slapped across the face. "I didn't mean that," he said.

"Whatever." I walked out of the room. I found Callie upstairs in her bedroom with a mickey of Jack Daniels in her hand. "Oh no," I moaned. "Not you too."

"What's up?" she asked, grinning. Her eyes were glossy and kept rolling around.

"Stay here," I ordered. I went to go find someone to help me. I found Connor, who was sober like me and more than willing to aid to Callie's need.

"You should probably go find Matt," Connor said.

"Why?"

"Last I saw him he was shotgunning beers in the back yard."

"What's his deal?" I was getting angry. I didn't understand why my boyfriend was being such a chalk head.

"I don't know, Aria," Connor said sympathetically, "but he better pray coach doesn't find out or he's a dead man." He arched his head towards Callie. "Same goes for this little lady here."

"You're pretty," Callie said to Connor, "but I like someone else." I rolled my eyes.

"I'll be back in a minute and then I can get her into bed. Can you help me start getting people out of here?" Connor nodded in response and I went to go find Matt. I should have just gone home. I kept telling myself this over and over again. This night didn't look like it was going to end positively.

Matt was sitting in the back yard on the lawn. A few kids were drinking and smoking by him. I went for the kids first. In my most authoritative voice, I told them that the police were on their way and they needed to leave. This cleared the yard almost instantly, and then I approached him.

"Can we talk?"

He nodded. His face was flushed and pale. I was happy to see he didn't appear to have any alcohol on him. "I'm sorry." The words were out of his mouth before I could even speak.

"Okay." I didn't really know what else to say. I was still irritated.

"It's okay?"

I sighed. "I don't know. What's wrong with you?"

"I went to the doctor today." Matt kicked the ground with his shoe. "My arm isn't healing properly. He thinks I might need surgery. Which means I might not be able to play ball this season. This means no scholarship and stuck at Jordan Falls Community College."

I didn't know what to say. I knew baseball meant the world to Matt. I tried to imagine having to sit out a season of basketball. I couldn't. But it still didn't give him an excuse to turn into a wild child. "When will they know for sure?"

"I have to get some more tests Monday," he said. He ran his fingers through his hair. "I was just really mad and needed to blow off some steam so Logan handed me a drink and the whole thing kind of snowballed."

"I think throwing away your morals for Logan is pretty stupid. So every time something doesn't go your way now, you're just going to pick up a bottle?"

He raised his eyebrows. "I think that's a little melodramatic."

"Oh, do you?"

"Come on, Aria," he said. He reached out and tucked a piece of my hair behind my ear. Then he smiled at me.

"Don't think you can just smile and make it better," I slapped his hand away from my face.

"I said I was sorry. Come on, give me a break. You know how much baseball means to me."

I could feel rage beginning to boil before I spoke. "You know what I like about you Matt? I like that you are different then other guys. That you aren't a typical jock. I like that you are a great big brother, that you go to church every weekend instead of getting smashed. But when you act like this, I just don't know."

His face fell. "I don't know what to say. I don't want to be like that."

"Then don't." I gave him a small smile. I'm not sure what he was thinking. He leaned forward and started to kiss me. I pulled back. "What are you doing?"

"Kissing my girlfriend?"

"Don't."

"Why not?" Matt was getting frustrated.

"Because I'm still annoyed at you." I crossed my arms.

"Can you stop being annoyed at me, please?" He smiled at me and poked my stomach. "Come on Aria." I shook my head at him and he began to tickle me. I fell to the ground in laughter as he continued to tickle me.

"Stop! Stop!" I breathed through my laughter.

"Say you forgive me?"

I kissed him on the lips. I started to pull away when he pulled me back towards him into a deep kiss. I could taste the liquor and cinnamon on his tongue. His mouth was hot. Matt had never kissed me like this before. I felt like our mouths were going to start a fire with the friction that was between them. Matt's hands travelled all over my body as he kissed me even harder. His hands went down my breasts slowly and I found myself so caught up in him that I couldn't even think. His hand found my belt buckle and he slowly began to unbuckle it.

I immediately pulled my lips away from him and sat up. "What are you doing?"

"I was just trying to have some fun."

My eyes just about shot out of my head. "Did you really think we were going to go at it in Callie's backyard?"

"No," he said. "I didn't. Ah. Look, I'm sorry."

"Seems to be a new pattern for you doesn't it." I readjusted my belt.

Matt sighed. "I don't know what you want from me," he said.

"I want you to get it together and start acting like the guy I fell in love with."

He muttered something under his breath that I didn't catch. I stood up. "I'm going inside," I said. "I'll see you later." I walked back towards the house leaving, Matt alone on the lawn.

Callie's house was a nightmare inside. Empty liquor bottles and drunken teenagers were scattered everywhere. I went upstairs and found the bathroom line. I stood impatiently waiting for my turn, still baffled by Matt's behaviour. I didn't know how to react to his new ways and I really hoped they weren't becoming a pattern.

I was so distracted that I didn't notice the sloshed girl coming out of the bathroom. She weaved her way down the hall and fell into the guy standing into front of me. He turned and spilt his cup of what I'm assuming wasn't just coke all over my top and pants.

"Great," I muttered.

"I'm so sorry!" he exclaimed.

"I really wish people would stop saying that to me." I looked up and saw a guy I recognized from one of my classes standing in front of me. I struggled to recall his name. Eli? Ezra?

"Here, let me grab you some towels." He grabbed a roll of paper towel nearing its shelf life off the floor and passed me some. "I'm so sorry," he said again.

"It's not your fault," I told him.

205

"You're Aria, right?" He asked. "I'm Ephram." Close enough. "We have physics together."

"We do." I glanced down at my clothes, still covered in pop.

"Here, let me help," Ephram grabbed some towel and tried to mop up some of the drink that had dissolved into my jean leg.

"Thanks," I said. I started to laugh. "Man, this is not my night." I don't really know what happened next. I was looking at Ephram who was about to speak when all of the sudden he went flying into the wall.

I turned and saw Matt's fist, which had just pummeled into Ephram's face. "Stay away from my girlfriend!" Matt yelled.

My eyes went wide. "What the hell is your problem?" I reached out and helped Ephram to his feet. "I'm so sorry."

"Hey no sweat," Ephram smiled weakly at me and looked at little queasy as he eyed Matt. "Sorry man, I was just trying to help her out."

"Well don't," Matt scowled.

"I can't even handle you." I walked down the stairs towards the front door.

"Where are you going?" Matt called after me.

"Away from you," I yelled back. I walked through the house, stepping over the bottles and garbage. I opened the front door and stepped outside. I heard the door close behind me. I spun around to look at Matt. "I don't want to talk to you right now, Matt."

"Aria –"

"I can't believe you. You just punched out a guy for no reason. What is your problem?"

"I'm sorry." He looked at me with sad eyes.

I took a deep breath. "I don't think we should see each other anymore."

"You don't mean that," he whispered.

"I'll see you around." I turned my back on him and began taking deep breaths as I made my way down the hall to Callie's room. Connor was sitting on the floor with Callie who looked like she was going to pass out any second.

"What's wrong?" Connor asked. He stood up and pulled up Callie with him.

I shook my head. "I just want to get out of here. How's she doing?"

"Better," Connor said. "I gave her lots of water and some Advil. I think she just needs to sleep it off."

"Thanks," I sighed. "Look, I really need to get out of here but I can't leave Callie here with all these people."

"I can take care of that," Connor grinned, "How about you get our princess here to bed and I'll take care of the rest?" That I could do.

I helped get Callie into her pajamas and tucked her into her bed; she had passed out before I even turned out the lights. Downstairs, Connor had told everyone the police were on their way. The place was empty in about two seconds. I looked around the house; it was completely trashed. My emotions started to spiral out of control. I felt a hand on my arm; I spun around, clenching my fists expecting to find Matt.

I found a concerned looking Connor instead. "Go home," he told me. "I'll clean up."

"I can't leave you like this," I mumbled. My eyes were burning and I could feel them starting to brim over with tears.

"Go," he said. "You look like you need to get out of here. I've got this."

"Thank you." Our eyes met for a second and then I turned and ran out of Callie's house and across her lawn to my own. I shook in the cold and felt my eyes start to water. I brushed the tears from my eyes and told myself I would not cry.

I opened the front door to the house and tried to be a quiet as possible letting myself in. It was still early, not even eleven. I prayed that Mom and Robert were already asleep and that I wouldn't have to deal with parents. The hall light flicked on. So much for that thought. Mom's slim figure was standing in the kitchen doorway, peering at me.

"Hi," I said, slipping off my shoes and putting them in the front closet.

"How was the girl's night?" Her voice had a strange tone that I was familiar with, saying, 'I know you lied and now I'm going to try and guilt you into being honest with me Mom tone.'

"Fine." I began to avert my eyes to the floor and caught myself quickly. "We played –"

Mom didn't even let me finish. "Don't lie to me, Aria."

"What?" I was surprised she had caught on that quickly.

She shook her head at me. "I can tell you're lying before the words even come out of your mouth."

"How?"

Mom sighed. "Oh no," she said. "I'm not giving that one up." She walked over to me, her eyes scrutinizing my clothing. She sniffed the air. "Is that beer I smell?"

I took a deep breath. "I wasn't drinking."

"That's not what I asked."

I sighed. "Yes, it is."

Mom put her right index finger to her right temple and rotated it slowly. A sign she was getting a headache. "Aria, we've talked about –" But she didn't even finish her sentence before I burst into tears. The tears came slowly at first and then quickly turned into loud, hyperventilating sobs.

A wave of worry washed over Mom's face. She immediately wrapped her arms around me. I sank into her hug and rested my head under her chin, crying as hard as I had ever cried in my life. When my sobs finally started dissolving, Mom led me into the living room and sat me down on the couch.

She started to speak and then stopped herself, studying my face instead. "Do you want to talk about it?" she finally asked.

"I…I…" I could barely get the words out. "I broke up with Matt." The tears began to fall down my face again. I told her the whole story through my sobs about how Matt had been drinking and what had happened outside – well almost all of that – and the fight at the end. Mom didn't say anything. She just rocked and cuddled and let me get it all out. When I finally finished talking, I looked up at her, waiting.

"He sounds confused," she said.

"I don't know what's wrong with him."

"How do you feel?"

I thought about this for a moment. "Like someone ripped my heart out of my chest and stomped on it."

"Ouch." Mom ran her fingers through my hair. I was waiting for her to comment on Matt's behaviour. To say that I deserved better and had done the right thing by leaving, but she didn't seem to be siding with anyone. "My poor baby," she cooed "it will be okay."

I don't know what it was about those four last words but they did the trick. Mom wasn't the type of person to tell me it was going to be okay if it wasn't.

I began to cry again. "I feel like I can't breathe without him, Mom." She hushed me once more until my crying subsided. I sat there in a state of shock and numbness. I could not believe what I had just done, and had no idea if I could ever put back together again.

Spring

19.

Matt and I were apart for over four weeks, although to me it felt more like years. The weekend of Callie's party had passed and Matt and I had both returned to school. No phone calls, no apologies, none of anything. I was hurt and surprised. The first Monday back at school, he didn't so much as even glance my way in the cafeteria. I left school after lunch and spent three hours bawling in Mom's office with her consoling me.

I tried to avoid him. We didn't have any classes together, so that wasn't as hard as I thought. But I would walk down the hall and hear his voice. See his tall figure from a mile away. Hear his laugh echoing across the cafeteria. I didn't know how he could laugh. I couldn't. I felt numb. So I did the only thing I could think of: I hid.

I became absorbed in my studies. Basketball season was over. Our team placed first in provincials, and both Callie and I had been scouted by some top-notch schools. But none of this mattered to me. I missed Matt. I missed him so much I could hardly think about anything else. I felt like the world was spinning around me and I was standing still watching.

The first week of March, Callie found me in the library during lunch. "What are you doing after school?" she asked.

"Homework." I didn't look up from my calculus textbook. The one good thing that came from not having a boyfriend anymore was my straight-A record. You'd think this would make my mom and Robert happy, but no. Instead, I had the psychologist mother and step-father who were more concerned that I wasn't dealing with my emotions properly, trying to smother me. I felt like I was close to breaking.

"We are all going to go cheer the guys on during baseball tryouts," Callie said. "You should come."

"No." I didn't even glance at her.

Callie grabbed the pencil from my hand. "Hey!" I yelled.

"I'm tired of this."

"Good for you?"

"Aria, come on."

I gave her a death glare. "Why would you think I would want to go to baseball try outs?"

"He's doing better."

"Callie, I don't want to hear it."

"He asks about you all the time."

"Well he has a phone," I said angrily.

Callie shook her head in disbelief. "Aria, Matt thinks you hate him. Come today. Talk to him. Stop doing this to yourself. You and Matt are the perfect couple and everyone knows it. He only has eyes for you."

"I have a lot of homework, Cal," I said, taking the pencil back from her. "Maybe next time."

"Okay, fine," she agreed. I didn't expect her to give up so easily. "Next time." She waved at me and left the library. That was very uncharacteristic of the Callie Jeakins I knew, but I decided to take it.

At the end of the day, after gathering up my pile of textbooks, I decided to stop by the baseball field. I don't know why I thought it would be a good idea, but I clearly wasn't thinking at the time. I wandered down the hallways to the south side of the school, pushed open the glass doors that lead me back to the track and playing fields and slowly made my way over to the baseball diamond.

When I saw him, my heart broke all over again. He wasn't alone. He was leaning against the chain fence talking to a girl. I had no idea who the girl was, but I had never seen her in my life. She was pretty – and she looked younger than us. Matt was talking and she was laughing. I stood absolutely still. Frozen. My brain tried to process, but it couldn't. He had moved on. Had he? I didn't know. I turned away from the scene, trying to ignore the tightness in my chest and fight off the tears that were forming.

I walked the long way home from school, my mind going a hundred miles a minute. I missed him. Even though he had been right in front of me, I missed him even more. It was like standing in front of a candy shop window and begging your Mom to let you have your favourite candy, but she says no – "It will spoil your dinner." So you just sit there instead, staring at the candy and wishing it was yours to have.

Missing Matt seemed to make me miss Dad even more. Robert and I were doing a little better these days and I didn't hate him anymore, but he would still never be my dad and I wasn't knocking on his door for advice either. My anger towards Matt had passed. I had been watching him enough to known that he indeed was doing better. He had gotten his cast off and had been working out regularly and was good to go for baseball season. An ecstatic Callie had shared the news with me a few weeks ago. She had however failed to mention the new love interest. It bothered me that the two of them had talked, but they'd known each other forever, so who was I to say anything?

As I walked, I tried to convince myself that it was all in my head. That I was exaggerating. Being overdramatic. I'm sure Matt had plenty of friends who were girls, just like I had friends who were guys. It wasn't a big deal. Right? Right. Just because I saw Matt with another girl didn't mean they were dating. It didn't mean anything. I hated those paranoid girls that always assumed their boyfriends were cheating on them for having a conversation with another girl. Hence my original reaction when Matt punched out Ephram at the party. I just felt horrible seeing him with someone else. Maybe because deep down, I really hadn't thought Matt and I were over. But now the hope was gone and it was time to accept our fate.

As soon as I got home I headed for the fridge. I made myself a massive banana split with all the toppings you could imagine and sat down at the table devouring it. I felt a little better after that. I pulled out my school books and started my English Lit paper. I was so engrossed in my writing that I didn't even hear the front door open. I looked up to see Mom, Robert, Quinn and Jeremy walk into the kitchen together. Quinn and Jeremy were holding hands.

I hadn't talked to Quinn much over the last month. She and Jeremy had gotten back together around the time Matt and I broke up. Needless to say, we didn't have a whole lot to talk about these days.

Mom sat down at the table beside me. "Hello, sweetheart."

"Hey." I looked at Quinn who looked like she was going to burst or something. "Are you okay?"

"We have an announcement," Quinn smiled. "Jeremy proposed and I said yes! We are getting married!"

I took a deep breath and decided not to be selfish. I stood up smiling and gave Quinn a big hug and then quickly grabbed her left hand to check out her bling. "Congrats, Quinnie! That is great; I'm really excited for you both." I tried to keep smiling, convincing myself that if I smiled long enough eventually it wouldn't be so hard to keep myself together.

We spent the next hour discussing weddings. For the most of it, I actually enjoyed myself. Quinn asked me to be her maid of honour. They were thinking of having an October wedding, as Quinn thought that autumn would be a very romantic time to get married. We discussed dates and venues – perhaps maybe September instead of October so they could have it outside. I was a role model sister through all of this. Even though my heart was hurting, I didn't need to rain on everyone else's parade.

Quinn and Jeremy were going out for dinner and Mom headed to her office to do some paper work. That left Robert and I for dinner. Yippee.

"Want to go out?" Robert asked. "Order in?"

I looked down at my paper and began leafing through my notes. "I'm not really hungry."

"Okay, well I'm going to order pizza and you can eat later if you feel like it."

"Sure."

"Aria, are you okay?" Here we go.

"I'm fine," I said, rolling my eyes.

"Aria," Robert pursed his lips. "Why don't you just talk to Matt and try to resolve your conflict? It's clearly upsetting you."

"I just need to finish this okay?" I felt my eyes start to water. I rubbed them with my fists. Robert nodded. The phone rang and he answered it.

"It's for you," he whispered. "Callie."

I let out an exaggerated sigh and took the phone. "Hey."

"What are you doing?" Callie's voice was chipper on the other line.

"Homework. How was baseball?"

"Fine," she said, continuing on. "Can we meet for coffee later?"

"Why?"

"Because I want to talk to you. We never see each other anymore."

"We have three classes together, you see me all the time."

"Please, Aria," she pleaded. "It's important."

I sighed. "Okay. Only for a bit though, okay? Where am I meeting you?"

"Jay's in an hour." Her parents' restaurant.

"Do you want to just walk together?"

"I'm at the library, so I'll just meet you."

"Sure, see you then."

"Bye."

I hung up the phone and found Robert studying my face. "Callie wants to go for coffee in an hour," I told him "She needs to talk or something."

"Is everything okay?" Robert asked, concerned.

"She probably just needs my opinion on a new hair style or something."

Robert laughed. "Callie's a nice girl."

"She's something alright," I shook my head. "Can I take the car?"

"I have to stop in at the hospital and check on a patient for a bit. I can drop you on my way. Just don't be out too late, okay?"

"Trust me," I told him, "I want to get home faster than you could imagine."

An hour later I was in a booth at Jay's waiting for Callie who was already five minutes late. I glanced around impatiently, wishing that I had brought some homework along. Looking around the restaurant, I noticed Matt sitting at the bar by the window. I hadn't seen him come inside. Our eyes met for a second and I quickly looked down at the table. I sat there for a few more minutes wondering where Miss I-need-to-talk was.

"Have you seen Callie?"

I looked up and saw Matt standing in front of me. I stared at him and wet my lips.

"Aria?"

"What?"

"Are you okay?"

I stared at him again and didn't say anything. I was at a loss for words. We hadn't spoken in four weeks.

"Callie asked me to meet her here," Matt explained. "But she's not picking up her phone and I haven't seen her."

"Callie asked me to meet her here too…" My voice slowly trailed off as I connected the dots. "Really?"

"What?" Matt looked confused. He always had been a little slow.

"This is a set up," I explained.

Matt watched me very closely for a moment, like I was a glass doll that had just been placed in his hands and could break any moment. Then he grinned and slid into the booth across from me.

"What are you doing?"

"What I should have done four weeks ago. Aria, I'm in love with you. I'm sorry I was an idiot. I don't know what I was thinking. I don't even know who that guy was. Whoever he was, I'm not him. I don't even know where he came from."

I didn't know what to say. 80 per cent of me wanted to jump up on the table and start getting my groove on. The other 20 was afraid. Afraid of the way Matt had behaved. Afraid he might do it again. I didn't want to keep getting hurt; my heart had been through enough.

"I thought you were seeing someone else," I confessed.

He did a double take. "What? Who?"

"I saw you with some girl yesterday at the baseball diamond."

He looked confused for a moment, then it clicked. "Oh! Her. She's in my fitness class. She was just asking me something about our exam next week."

"Oh." I didn't really know what else to say. I felt like a moron.

"I know what you're thinking," he continued. "You don't know if you can trust me again. Aria, I promise you if you give me one more chance, I won't let you down. You're it, Aria. You're the one. When you aren't in my life, there's nothing left for me."

My knees started shaking under the table. I looked into Matt's blue eyes and instantly felt safe again. I believed him. As scared as I was, I was miserable without Matt. No one had ever made me feel the way he did. When I was with him, it felt like the best versions of both of us were entwined into one whole.

I reached across the table and took both his hands into mine. "I love you too, Matt." I smiled and, for the first time in a long time, it was authentic.

Matt whooped for joy. Literally. He jumped out of the booth picked me up and spun me around in the air gleefully.

"Matt," I hissed. "Everyone's watching!"

"So let them." He grinned and parted his lips. The moment our lips touched, I felt a jolt of electric current run through my body. All of my senses awakened to his touch. It was a moment that belonged in utopian bliss.

Matt and I spent the next hour snuggled up in a booth together. It felt exactly the way it did before. "Are you going to come watch me try out tomorrow?" he asked. He took his finger tip and traced the edges of my lips.

"Definitely," I smiled. "I can't wait to see you play. And your arm is good?"

"It's perfect," he said. "Not even a bit sore."

"That's great."

Matt drove me home a while later. He walked me to the front door and kissed me goodbye. I clung to him for an extra moment. "I don't want to wake up tomorrow and have this all be a dream," I explained.

"I promise it's not. I'll pick you up tomorrow morning?"

"Okay."

"Bye." He kissed me on the forehead and jogged down the walkway to his truck.

Inside the house I skipped into the kitchen. Mom and Quinn were talking at the table.

"Guess what?" I practically shouted. They both eyed me suspiciously.

"What?" Quinn played along.

"Matt and I got back together," I sang. I hopped from one foot to another with a massive grin on my face.

Quinn broke out into a smile. "That's awesome, Aria."

"I'm happy for you," Mom chimed it. "When did this happen?"

"Callie set us up," I explained. "I wasn't really meeting Callie for coffee. She sent Matt instead."

"How television," Quinn remarked.

"I thought it was cute!"

"It is," she agreed. "I'm glad you are happy again. I wasn't a fan of sulky, nose-glued-to-a-textbook Aria."

"Me neither," Mom laughed.

"Well she's gone for good!" I considered this. "Well, maybe not the-nose-in-a-textbook part. My grades really liked her."

Mom shook her head at me. "How about you just find a balance?"

"Deal." I looked at the table for the first time since I had entered the room. It was covered with bridal magazines. "Planning already?"

"Just looking," Quinn blushed. "Nothing wrong with getting a head start."

I pulled up a chair. "So what are we looking at?" Quinn handed me a magazine and I entered into a world of cakes, flowers and long flowing dresses.

20.

The next morning I woke up feeling like it was Christmas morning. I took extra time getting ready for school. I wore the green sweater Matt loved on me – the one he said brought out my eyes. I also curled my hair; I knew how much he loved playing with my curls. When I looked in the mirror before heading downstairs, I was satisfied with the end result.

The doorbell rang. I raced down the stairs and flung open the front door. Matt stood on the porch, a bouquet of flowers in his hands.

"You didn't have to get me flowers!" I exclaimed.

"You're supposed to say thank you." He wiggled his eyebrows at me and I laughed. He handed me the flowers. Gerber daisies in a beautiful arrangement of purple, pink and off-white. They were beautiful. I told him so. He responded by taking me in his arms and holding me closely. We stood like that for a minute or two. I had forgotten how good it felt to be in Matt's arms.

"We should get going," he said, interrupting my thoughts.

"I'd rather just stay here all day," I protested.

"Me too."

At school, we were wonderfully back in sync. Matt held my hand as we walked down the hallway; he carried my books for me and walked me to my first class of the day, where he said he could hardly wait until lunch to see me. It felt too good to be true; part of me kept wanting to pinch myself to see if I was dreaming or not.

I met Callie in calculus, our first class of the day. She was beaming at me and Matt in the hall from her seat. I sat down beside her.

She smiled. "So I take it yesterday went well?"

"I can't believe you did that." I rolled my eyes at her.

"Are you mad?" A look of concern spread over her face. "I thought you would be ha –"

"Thank you," I interrupted.

"What?"

"I'm not mad. It probably needed to be done. You are a good friend, Callie, and I really appreciate it. I was a mess without him."

"I know," she twirled a piece of her black hair around her finger. "I'm glad you are happy again."

"Me too."

After school, Callie and I took our books down to the baseball diamond to study together and watch the boys try out. It was warm for March. T-shirt weather already. I was used to snow all the way up until April, but this was a change I could definitely get used to. We sat in the middle row of the old wooden bleachers, which has a structure that slightly concerned me. The bleachers looked like they were being supported by a small pinky finger and could collapse at any moment.

I warily took a seat beside Callie and pulled out my physics textbook.

"I'm having trouble with number seven," I said, opening my book to our homework questions. "Can you help me?"

"Sure." Callie opened her book to the same page, scanned the page and then launched into a long discussion that was a foreign language to me.

"Hm." I blinked my eyes quickly at her and then closed my book. "Maybe I need a bit of a homework break. What are you doing this weekend?"

"Flying to Montreal with Mom and Dad."

"For?" I raised my eyebrows. That didn't seem like your typical weekend trip.

"We are going to see McGill's campus." A prestigious eastern university.

"Already?"

"Aria!" Callie shook her head at me. "We are going to be graduating soon. It's important to have a plan."

"I guess so." My mind wandered away from her and my eyes looked over to Connor and Matt playing catch on the field. "I'm just excited that I get to spend the weekend with Matt."

Callie's eyes twinkled. "I bet. What are you guys doing?"

"Friday night we are going out somewhere – he won't tell me where. It's our six-month anniversary, apparently."

Callie's mouth formed an "O" shape. "But you broke up?"

"Yeah," I laughed. "That was my argument, but he insisted. I think Matt's more of a girl than me when it comes to stuff like that. Saturday we are probably spending the day together and he said they have a baseball kick-off thing with the guys at night."

"Oh yeah," Callie rolled her eyes. "The famous kick-off."

"Famous? Why?"

"It's just always top secret what they do."

I frowned. "Well that's slightly concerning."

Callie laughed. "I'm sure it's harmless. I think they just like to keep us guessing."

"Probably." I rolled my eyes at her and opened my textbook again. "Okay, what about question 10?"

Callie flipped to question 10 and began reading. I sighed. It felt like graduation couldn't come soon enough.

I was given no details for our six-month anniversary. Well, Matt told me to wear something comfortable. I told him this as a risky statement, for all he knew I could show up in a pair of sweat pants and a wife beater. He laughed at this and said I would still look beautiful anyways. My Prince Charming.

Matt told me to meet him at his house at 5 o'clock sharp. I booked it home from school, showered and changed my clothes. I aimed to look casual but cute in dark jeans, a flowery patterned shirt and a gray cardigan. Besides, I had a slight suspicion that we were going to be staying at Matt's house, or at least close to home. He always picked me up for a date, so I found it strange that a guy who had been obsessing all week about our anniversary had told me to meet him at his house.

His parents had gone on a ski trip for spring break. The little kids got an extra week; ours didn't start for another week, which I thought was extremely unfair. High school – especially senior year – should account for more than one week of spring break. I had been making this argument to just about anyone who would listen. So far, no one seemed to sympathize with my pain.

Quinn was working a night shift at the hospital and dropped me off at Matt's house on her way. He opened the door looking as gorgeous as ever in a pair of jeans and a fitted black t-shirt. I glanced down at my own wardrobe selection. It seemed I had made the right choice. He then ushered me inside into the kitchen, my eyes opened wide at what was before me.

Matt had transformed the kitchen. The table was set with a beautiful white table cloth on it and two place settings. Red rose petals were scattered over it and candles were lit all over the room. Soft music played in the background. Lying at the head of the table was a beautiful arrangement of red roses. I walked over and picked them up.

"Those are for you," Matt said, resting his hand on my arm.

"They are beautiful."

"You are beautiful."

I picked up the small card that had been perched next to the flowers and read it: *"Aria, you are truly the most amazing person I have ever met. Being with you is simply enchanting. Always and forever. Love, Matt."*

My heart was pounding. I looked around the room and was at a loss for words. I loosely draped my arms around Matt's neck.

I smiled at him. "Have I told you how much I love you?"

"I've missed hearing it," he admitted.

"We'll I guess we have some making up to do." I kissed him fiercely, wanting to be as close to him as possible. He sunk into the kiss. I wondered how we had ever thought we could be apart.

The evening was a fairytale. Matt cooked us steak, potatoes and grilled vegetables (my favourite) for dinner. The food tasted incredible. After dinner, I discovered he had stored one of my bathing suits away. We went in the hot tub where he served us sparkling apple juice and charmed me even more than imaginable. We ended the night snuggling in front of the fireplace, eating a delicious chocolate cheesecake that Matt had made himself. This guy was full of surprises. I was half expecting him to pull out a horse-drawn carriage when it was time to take me home.

He didn't, surprisingly. On the ride home it started to rain and Matt pulled off to the side of the road.

"What are you doing?" I asked, uneasily.

"Get out of the truck," he said. He opened his door and stepped out of the truck.

"Why?" I bit my lip. It was now pouring rain outside.

"I want to dance with you." Matt was smiling from ear to ear.

"You want to do what?" I was staring at him like he was insane.

"Look, I have this list. A bucket list. One of the things on it is to dance with a beautiful girl in the rain. So, shall we?"

I laughed. Then I realized he was serious. He ran around to my side of the truck, flung open my door and carried me out into the rain.

It was crazy. I was laughing and shaking my head at him, getting completely drenched at the same time. "There's no music," I informed him.

"Hold on a second." He jogged back to the truck and cranked up the stereo as loud as it would go. The words to Taylor Swift's "Fearless" drifted my way. Matt raced back over to me. "Happy?"

"Ecstatic." I watched the raindrops fall lightly on his face. He grabbed my hands and spun me out and away from him. I giggled madly as he pulled me close again. "Has anyone ever told you that you are completely insane?"

"That's why you love me," he smiled. "It's called living in the moment." We swayed to the music for a long time. It was beautiful. I think that was the moment I knew without a doubt I was going to marry Matt Lawson. It didn't matter that we hadn't graduated from high school, that we were only 17 and still needed to get through college. He was it for me.

We got back to my house just before midnight. We were both completely soaked. Matt had driven with his free arm around my shoulders, trying to keep me from shivering. I kissed him goodnight, told him I loved him and sprinted into the house. I needed warmth. No one was home yet. Mom and Robert had gone out for dinner and to a show in town. It looked like they were having a late night as well.

Once in my bedroom, I stripped off my soaking wet clothes and ran a steaming hot bath. After a few minutes of being in the water, I began to regain feeling in my fingers and toes. When I felt I had reached a normal temperature, I hopped out of the tub and put on a pair of Matt's pajama pants I had stolen from him, along with a tank top. I climbed into my bed, feeling exhausted. I was out like a light the minute I closed my eyes and slept soundly until morning.

21.

I awoke the next morning sneezing. I couldn't recall ever waking up sneezing in my lifetime. I sat up in bed, instantly regretting it and wanting to lie back down again. My throat felt scratchy, and I couldn't breathe through my nose. I had a cold. Great. My cell phone rang on the nightstand next to my bed.

"Hello?" I croaked. It was Matt.

"You sound horrible," he said. "Don't move, I'll be right over." I fell back into my threshold of pillows and waited for my knight to show up.

Half an hour later, Matt came into my room with a bowl of chicken noodle soup in one hand, a bottle of cough medicine in the other and Mom trailing behind him with a thermometer. Mom took my temperature and fussed over me until I assured her I was fine. When it showed I didn't have a fever, she left me with Matt. This surprised me; Mom wasn't one to leave me alone in my room with a boy, although she left the door wide open.

"I feel so bad," Matt said after I finished my soup. "I shouldn't have made you freeze your butt off in the rain."

I smiled at him. "It was worth it. I mean, I couldn't be the reason you didn't get to achieve your dreams in life."

"True story."

We spent the rest of the afternoon play board games and drinking tea. Matt schooled me at Uno, Checkers and

Go Fish. I did however beat him at Old Maid, which he claimed to be a fitting name. This remark earned him a massive red welt on his arm. He then sat beside me and played with my hair – one of my favourite things to have done when I was sick. Around dinner time, he told me he had to go.

I was disappointed but was also feeling much better. "Can't you just stay a bit longer?" I pleaded and stuck out my lower lip in a pout.

He made a sad face back at me. "I can't babe. It's initiation for the new guys on the team tonight and I have to be there. But maybe I'll be able to stop by again later and check in on you if you're still up."

"Okay." I gave him a small smile. He leaned in to kiss me and I pulled back. "I don't want you to get sick."

"I've been with you all day," he reasoned. "If I'm going to get sick, it won't be from one kiss." He kissed me quickly on the lips and gave me a hug. "Feel better, baby. I'll call you later."

I was bored as soon as he left. I went downstairs and ate dinner with Mom and Robert, then decided to get started on my mounds of homework. I took some more cold medicine, covered my upper body in Vicks and began my calculus homework.

I started to drift off to sleep around 9 o'clock. I closed my textbook and drowsily found my way to my bed. The next thing I knew, I was being gently shaken by Mom.

"Aria, sweetheart," her voice was soft, "wake up."

I sat up, feeling completely disillusioned. My eyes fluttered open and shut for a few seconds before finding their way to my alarm clock. It was just after midnight. I looked into Mom's eyes and saw a flash of worry within them. I suddenly felt like I had just been punched in the stomach.

"What's wrong?" I asked.

Mom's face fell. She put her hand on my arm. "Sweetie, I just got off the phone with Matt's mom. There was an accident and he's in the hospital. We should go there now."

Everything from that moment forward was a complete blur. I changed into some clothes and Robert drove us to the hospital. When I asked Mom what happened and if he was okay, she told me we should wait until we got there to find out more. Not the answer I wanted to hear.

We got to the hospital in record time and Mom took me to the trauma unit, while Robert parked the car. I kept taking deep breaths. We walked through a set of glass doors and I saw Connor and some guys sitting in the waiting room. Connor was hunched over with his face buried in his hands. I ran over to him and he stood up the moment he saw me, pulling me into a tight embrace.

"What happened?" My mouth felt dry and I wet my lips. "Is he okay?"

"Aria," Connor's voice seemed to fumble over his words. "I'm so sorry. I don't know how it happened. I don't know."

"Connor," I said his name again. He just stared at me, unable to speak. Matt's dad came into the waiting room. Peter looked tired, his eyes red and sunken. He approached me.

"What happened?" I repeated the words again.

"There was a fight," he said. I carefully tuned my ears to absorb everything he was about to tell me. "I don't have the whole story yet, but from what the boys are saying they were up at the school when it happened. Apparently they were approached by a group of young men that began to harass Logan Banks."

"Logan." I said his name bitterly.

Peter looked confused at my reaction and I didn't say anything. "It got violent. From what I understand Matt tried to intervene. He got punched in the head and fell. His head hit the curb." Tears rolled down Peter's face as he spoke. I felt numb. "Aria, they are still running some more tests, but they are saying he is brain dead. He is nonresponsive right now and in a coma. He's not able to breathe on his own."

I felt dizzy. I couldn't understand. I didn't want to understand. I felt my knees began to give away. The room started spinning. My breathing was heavy. Mom grabbed me by the arm and Peter helped her sit me down in a waiting room chair.

"Put your head between your legs," Mom instructed. I did what she said. She rubbed my back slowly. "Take deep breaths," she coached. I did for a few minutes and then sat back up.

"I want to see him," I said.

"He doesn't look like himself, Aria," Peter warned me. "He is in really rough shape –"

"I want to see him," I interrupted. My words were free of any emotion.

Peter led me into Matt's room. Carol and Rachel stood by the bed, both had been crying. They enveloped me in hugs. Mom stood behind me with both her hands on my shoulders, as if she were trying to steady me.

My eyes wandered to the bed. Matt was lying in the bed, his tall legs hanging off the edge of it. My eyes finally found his face. Tubes were coming out of his mouth. IVs were inserted in both his arms. He had a fat lip; his face was red, swollen and covered in scratches. His head was wrapped in a large white bandage, which was stained with dried blood.

I moved over to him and took his hand in mine. It was warm. I didn't say anything. I couldn't. I just held his hand.

"Honey?" Mom's voice spoke from behind me. She handed me a tissue. I gave her a strange look, then put my free hand to my cheek. I didn't realize tears were flowing down my face.

"I want to stay with him," I said, turning to him. "Until he wakes up." Matt's mom started sobbing after I said this. I kept my eyes on Matt and didn't move.

Doctors and nurses came in and out of the room but I never left Matt's side. I don't know how long I sat there for. His parents left with the doctors and then they came back into the room with Mom and Robert. Quinn, clothed in hospital scrubs, entered a few minutes after. Quinn came over to me and put her arm around me.

"Hey sweetie." Her voice was light and calm. She was being careful, I could tell. "Can I talk to you for a minute?" I nodded, but never let go of Matt's hand and didn't take my eyes away from him. "Can we go outside?" I shook my head and began to cry. Quinn grabbed my free

239

hand. "You can come back in after, Aria. I promise. Okay?"

I nodded slowly. I let her unlink my hand from Matt's and she took me out into the hallway. Mom and Robert followed us.

"Aria," Quinn spoke very slowly and clearly. "I need to talk to you about Matt." I nodded. I didn't have any words to respond.

Robert handed me a glass of water. "Drink this." I did.

I studied Quinn's face. She looked conflicted, struggling to find the words. She turned to Mom. Mom took a deep breath. A cleansing breath, as she would have referred to it. Then Mom spoke but no words came out. Robert took over.

"Remember back in December when Matt got a concussion?" I didn't respond. Robert's words softly echoed in my head.

Quinn spoke this time. "The doctor's think that Matt obtained a blood clot from that concussion. He had a history of them and it's really the only explanation. The second he was punched tonight, he had what appears to be an aneurysm. That means that the clot in Matt's brain exploded and –" she stopped. "He was instantly brain dead."

Brain dead. The words were not registering in my head. What did that mean? Was he going to be okay? They could fix brain damage, couldn't they? I couldn't seem to get these questions out of my mouth. This moment was taking forever, and I just wanted to know if the love of my life was going to be okay.

240

Quinn's lower lip trembled slightly. "Aria, he can't breathe on his own and shows no sign of brain activity. There is no chance of recovery. They are going to take him off life support in the next hour." She paused, closed her eyes, then opened them again. She was teary. "The doctors want you all to say your last goodbyes."

My heart sunk to the floor. I felt the tears flowing down my face, but I couldn't believe Quinn. I shook my head at her. She was wrong. She had to be wrong. Matt was going to be fine. I kept telling myself this and walked back into his room with Mom and Quinn on my heels.

A few of the guys were huddled around Matt. They were all saying words of goodbye to him. Logan was nowhere to be seen. One by one they exited and just Connor was left. I watched Connor, tears streaming down his face. He had his hand on Matt's arm.

"I love you man," he whispered. "I'll hit you a home run to heaven." He squeezed his arm and turned to face me. He hugged me and began sobbing. I sank into his hug for a moment. Peter clasped his hand on Connor's shoulder and steered him out of the room. "Let's give Aria a minute alone with Matt," he said quietly.

I stood at the edge of Matt's bed, my heart pounding and my ears closed off to everything that was happening around me. I had a flashback of this same scene from the day that Dad had died. After that, I wasn't sure if my heart would ever feel whole again. It was Matt who had finally pieced it back together. What was I going to do now?

I lightly ran my fingertips over his face and took one of his hands with my other free one. "Don't leave me," I whispered. "I won't make it without you." I put my head down on his shoulder and tried to get as close to him as I could. It was awkward with all the machines. "We were supposed to be together forever. You can't leave me." I kissed him on the lips, but they didn't feel like his lips anymore. They were swollen and chapped. Hollow. This wasn't the way I wanted to remember him. "I love you," I whispered. "Always and forever." I began to cry, then I let go of his hand and ran.

I didn't know where I was running as I dashed out of Matt's room. I tore through the waiting room and began weaving in and out of the hallways. Tears were streaming down my face and I could hear hyperventilating sobs coming from my mouth. I found the glass entrance, ran past it and collapsed on the cement parking lot beside a light post. Everything was blurry. I took a deep breath and the sobs became silent.

I heard soft footsteps behind me and felt an arm go around my shoulders.

"I'm so sorry, Aria." Quinn's voice shook as she spoke.

I started screaming. I don't even know what words I was screaming and they didn't make any sense, even to me. I pulled away from Quinn and sat in the parking lot, yelling at the sky, asking why, how. That it wasn't fair. Why me? I stood up and kicked the metal railing that stood before me. I kicked and kicked until I was sobbing so hard I couldn't breathe. I dropped to the ground. I heard voices around me. Robert, Mom and Quinn.

"Maybe we should get one of the doctors to look at her," Quinn said in the background.

"We are doctors," Mom told her. Point taken. "She's in shock, honey. This isn't going to be easy on her. I'm going to take her home."

"Okay," Quinn said. "I'm going to talk to my supervisor and see if I can get off early."

Mom picked me up firmly by the arms. "Aria, sweetheart. Let's go home."

"I can't leave," I said in a mute tone that didn't sound like me.

"Honey," Robert said gently. "We need to get you home." I felt his arms go around my waist and hold me up with Mom. "You will feel better after you get some sleep."

Tears that I didn't even know I had left began to roll down my cheeks again. "I won't ever feel better."

Mom took me in her arms. She held me for a while and I continued to cry. Eventually she led me to the car and they drove me home.

I don't remember the ride home. One minute we were at the hospital and the next minute Mom was walking me up to my room and putting me to bed. She took my temperature, then my blood pressure and gave me a sleeping pill. I curled up in a ball under my comforter and hugged a pillow close to my body, wishing that it was Matt.

Mom sat down on my bed. "Can I get you anything?"

"I want Matt." I felt hollow, and the words sounded dead coming out of my mouth.

"I'm so sorry, sweetheart." Mom reached out for me but I pulled my blanket right over my head.

I didn't respond. I just wanted Matt. I wanted to feel his arms around me, his lips on mine. I wanted to see his face, with his beautiful blue eyes and his smile that could light up a room. I had never felt so empty before. I felt like my heart had been ripped out of my chest and stomped on a thousand times. I was completely broken. And the worst part was I didn't know who was going to help put me back together again.

The sleeping pills helped. I fell into a heavy, dreamless sleep. When I woke up, it was four in the afternoon the next day. The second I opened my eyes, I was hit with a wave of remembering. I felt my stomach churn like an empty pit. I didn't move from my bed. I lay there, staring at the ceiling, trying to feel something other than pain. Nothing happened.

Eventually Mom came into my room. She brought me some soup and a mug of hot tea. "How are you feeling?" she asked.

I closed my eyes again. I just wanted to be fine. To pretend. To feel something real. "I'm fine." I sat up in bed and smiled, but the fakeness hurt even more. "I just woke up. I was going to come find you."

Mom watched me wearily. I could see her eyes diagnosing me. I remember when Dad had died, Mom had told me about the seven steps of grieving. Denial, guilt, anger, depression, the "upward turn" (her favourite), reconstruction and acceptance.

"Matt's parents called," Mom said in a flat tone. "The funeral is going to be held on Wednesday." Funeral. The word slapped me in the face. I pushed it aside.

There was a knock on my door. Robert pushed it open. "Hey, you have a visitor." I looked over to see Callie.

"Omigosh!" she squealed when she saw me. "Aria! I'm so sorry. Are you okay? Oh no! Of course you're not okay! I don't know why I'm even asking you that!" She threw her arms around me. I hugged her back. "How are you doing though?"

"I'm okay," I shrugged and gave her a small smile.

"Really?" Callie eyed me suspiciously. "A bunch of people are going over to Connor's. Do you want to go? Just hang out and be with everyone."

"Sounds good," I said. I turned to Mom. "Can I go?"

"Are you sure you want to go out right now?" I recognized this tone. The I-really-don't-want-you-to-leave-but-I'm-going-to-let-you-make-your-own-choice-anyways tone.

"Yeah," I said. "Why wouldn't I?"

Mom sighed. "Just be home by 10." She gave me a quick hug. "I love you."

"You too." I turned to Callie. "Just give me 10 minutes to change and get ready."

"Take your time." Callie sat down on my bed.

Quite a few people were at Connor's house. Some girls from the basketball team and a bunch of Matt's friends from the baseball team. We met up in Connor's backyard. It was still light outside. The guys had started a small bonfire. I thought of the last bonfire I had attended, back when Matt and I first met. The memory hit me hard and almost knocked the wind out of me. I focused on breathing.

The second Connor saw me, his eyes filled with tears. He wrapped me in an embrace. "Aria, I didn't think you'd come."

"I didn't want to be alone," I admitted.

His eyes showed guilt. "I'm so sorry."

"It's not your fault. It was an accident."

"I know." He looked so sad. "Can I get you a drink or anything?"

"I'm okay right now. Thanks, though."

I spent the next hour receiving condolences from people. I felt like I was going to burst. I didn't want to talk. I wandered through Connor's backyard. Like Matt's, Connor's house was massive. His full-acre backyard had a pond, a large gazebo and many beautiful gardens. I walked down to the gazebo and sat on the swing.

Eventually Callie came and joined me. She didn't say anything for a while, which was nice. She just let me sit there in the quiet. She put her arm around me and I rested my head on her shoulder. Human contact felt amazing. It was the only thing that didn't make me feel like I was sinking into quicksand.

"Can you take me home?" I finally asked. "I'm tired."

Callie stood up. "Sure. Let's go."

We walked back towards the house, our arms linked together. We were almost back near the fire when I heard yelling. Callie broke into a run and I followed her. We got there just in time to see Connor throw a punch at Logan. Logan. I didn't know what Logan was doing here.

"It's all your fault!" Connor's yelled and before breaking out into a cry. "It's your fault he's dead!"

"I miss him too, man," Logan said quietly. His eyes looked tired.

"Connor," I walked over to him and held him by the arm. "Stop. Please, just stop. Remember why we're here."

Connor's eyes widened and his face went pale. "I'm sorry. I'm sorry."

I glanced at Logan, whose left eye was beginning to swell. "Cal – can you take Logan to get some ice for his eye?"

Callie shot me a glance. "Really?"

"Yes," I said sternly.

Logan looked at me. "Thank you." I didn't respond. I turned back to see Connor bawling like a baby and I went to comfort him.

Connor gritted his teeth. "Someone needs to pay for what happened to him."

"They will," I soothed. "You know they will. Have you talked to Matt's parents today?"

He told me he had. Connor informed me that the police were now fully investigating Matt's death – there was a possibility that it was going to be tried as a murder. They caught the boys who started the fight. Rumor was that it was possibly gang-related.

Connor told me more. Apparently a few months back, after everything had happened with his brother, Logan had gotten in trouble with a gang but somehow managed to get out – or so he thought. He had had some rough encounters with the same guys again; Matt and some of the guys from the team had been trying to help protect him.

My heart sank hearing this. I hadn't known anything of this, but putting his own life before his friends sure sounded like the Matt I knew. The Matt I loved.

When Callie came back, Logan was no longer with her or anywhere else that I could see. I left Connor in her care and then called Quinn for a ride home.

I waited in the driveway for Quinn. Too much drama happening for me to be around everyone else right now. I couldn't deal. A few minutes later, Robert pulled up in his truck. I quickly got in.

"How was your night?" he asked, carefully looking me over as if to see if I had picked up any bruises or wounds.

"It was fine. I thought Quinn was picking me up?"

"I offered," Robert said calmly. "Just fine?"

"I'm tired," I told him. "I just want to sleep."

"You know if you want to talk about it –"

"I don't."

"Aria," Robert's voice was gentle. "You can't pretend it didn't happen. Matt's dead."

I didn't respond. He didn't offer any more words of wisdom, which was wise because he likely would have been the second one to have a black eye tonight. I just wanted my bed. I went straight up to my room when we got home and was followed by Mom, of course.

"I don't want to talk," I told her. "I already told Robert. I just want to sleep."

She seemed to understand. She gave me another sleeping pill and helped me into bed. I closed my eyes and fell asleep instantly. This sleep, however, was not as forgiving as the last one. I tossed and turned most of the night. I felt anxious and stressed; sleep wasn't coming easily.

I got out of bed at five in the morning – Monday morning. I showered, did my hair, put on make-up, and dressed myself. I went downstairs and began pulling things out of the cupboards. I made eggs, bacon, hash browns, pancakes and waffles. Enough food to feed an army.

By the time breakfast was ready, the house had begun to stir. I heard Mom and Robert talking upstairs. Their room was just above the kitchen. I also heard Quinn running around, getting ready for work. I sat at the table full of food, not touching or eating any of it. Eventually they all came downstairs.

"What the heck?" Quinn was the first to speak. "Did you turn into Martha Stewart this morning?"

Robert smiled and sat down beside me. "Smells awesome, Aria."

Mom ignored the massive amount of food on the table. "I thought you were still sleeping, sweetie? How are you feeling?"

"Fine," I said. "Can you drive me to school?"

"Are you sure you're up for school today?" Robert asked through a mouthful of food. "This is great, by the way."

"Thanks," I began to nervously fiddle with my hair. "Yes, I'm ready. No point in sitting around here all day being sad."

"I don't think that was implied," Mom sighed, "but yes, I'll drive you. When do you want to leave?"

"Whenever you're done eating."

Mom drove me to school shortly after. She must have asked me about 10 times if I was sure I was okay and repeatedly told me to call her if I needed anything. I shrugged and got out of the car, staring at the large building in front of me. I took several deep breaths before I could go inside. I opened the glass doors at the front of the school and immediately felt like everyone was watching me. I heard the whispers. A few people came up to me and offered their condolences. I brushed them off.

I found my locker. I opened it and stared inside. I didn't even know which class I had first that day.

"What are you doing here?" I heard Callie's voice beside me. I closed my locker, not even noticing I hadn't taken out any books.

"I'm here for school," I said sarcastically.

"Well, clearly," Callie said. "I just mean, no one expected you to come today."

"It's fine."

"Okay," Callie's tone was hesitant; she didn't seem to believe me. The bell rang and we started walking to class. I began to relax and felt that maybe this wasn't going to be so bad after all. We turned a corner in the hallway and Callie stopped walking suddenly.

"What's wrong?" I started to say, but when my eyes saw what was in front of me, I didn't finish speaking. We were in front of Matt's locker. Matt's locker had been transformed. Covered with posters of his face plastered all over it. Cards. Teddy bears. Flowers.

A crowd of people huddled around the locker. Some were talking, others were crying and others were completely silent.

As I slowly walked towards his locker, the crowd parted like the Red Sea. I kneeled down and picked up a red rose lying on the floor. I held it to my nose and inhaled. Then I lost control. The scent of that flower hit my nostrils and every emotion I had been holding in suddenly exploded. I started sobbing loudly; the sobs sounded more like screams. I couldn't stop. I lost all control over my body.

Someone picked me up off the floor and ushered me to the office. I was told my mother was on her way, but I could not stop the tears. Callie sat there with me, looking helpless and afraid. When Mom rushed through the office doors, relief flooded Callie's face. The second I saw Mom, I flew into her arms before I could even blink.

It took her a while to calm me down, but eventually I was stable enough so she could take me home. I went upstairs to change my clothes and then came down to the kitchen where she was waiting for me.

"It hurts," I finally said. "I feel like half of me just got ripped away. Like I don't have a heart. Like everything good I ever felt with him is gone and multiplied into darkness. I can't breathe without him, Mom. It hurts so bad."

"I know it does, baby," she soothed. "It will get easier though, I promise. But Aria, you are not going to feel better overnight. You need to take baby steps."

I thought about the concept of baby steps. I had never been good at moving slowly. Always wanting to jump ahead and get to the next level. Patience was something that I lacked. I wasn't going to be able to just forget about Matt. He was a part of me. How was I supposed to move on without him?

22.

Matt's funeral was a week later at 11 o'clock in the morning. There was a graveside burial, followed by a celebration of life afterwards. The word "celebration" haunted me. I spent most of the morning freaking out. First I didn't like my hair, which Quinn helped me fix. Next, I went into a frenzy of what to wear. Did I need to wear all black? Mom said I didn't. I ended up choosing a black skirt, a green shirt – one of Matt's favourites – and a pair of heels. I couldn't eat anything. Mom tried to fight me on this one but eventually let it go.

We all drove to the funeral together. Mom, Robert, Quinn, Jeremy and myself. As we drove in I saw a long line of people – hundreds or people – walking towards Matt's grave. Mom took me over to Matt's family. Hugs and words exchanged.

It didn't feel real. I kept thinking that over and over to myself. That if I kept pinching myself I was going to wake up from this nightmare. The graveside ceremony felt eerie to me. I watched solemnly. Connor, Matt's two brothers and three guys from the baseball team were pallbearers, carrying the coffin from the hearse over to the grave. I just kept watching.

I saw Ruthie, Matt's younger sister, clinging to Rachel and her mom. My heart broke all over again. This little girl adored her big brother. To her, he was Superman. The guy who gave her piggy back rides, helped her build a snow man and taught her Sunday school class. The younger girl looked almost frozen, too young to understand completely what was happening, but terrified of what she could comprehend.

Matt's pastor spoke for a while. I listened. He welcomed everyone, which I thought was bizarre. Who actually wanted to be here? He began to talk about Matt, but I wasn't listening anymore. Everyone began to sing later. They were singing a hymn – a familiar one to me, and one of Matt's favourites. "Amazing Grace." I listened to the words. "I once was lost but now am found, was blind but now I see." They comforted me. I felt a small sliver of hope.

I closed my eyes as they lowered Matt's coffin into the ground. My heart was racing and my eyes were dry. The pastor announced that we could go and sprinkle dirt over Matt's coffin as a last "goodbye." His family went first. I followed them. I picked up the dirt in the palm of my hand. I approached the coffin and lightly sprinkled it over top. I expected to feel something – *anything*- but I just felt raw. I examined the coffin. Earlier, Robert had told me that they had to order an extra long coffin because Matt had been too tall to fit in a regular-sized one. Standing there now, this struck me as humourous. I chuckled softly to myself.

Mom eyed me nervously and led me back to the patch of grass we had been standing on. She put her arm around me. I was completely dry-eyed. The pastor said a final prayer and then invited us all back to the church to celebrate Matt's life together. Robert drove us all there. I couldn't help like feeling, though, that the graveside ceremony hadn't been enough.

The church was the hardest part. The same pastor who had spoken earlier gave a brief testimony of Matt's life. It was beautiful and highlighted him and his integrity well, but I found my eyes staring at the large picture of Matt on the overhead. His graduation picture, taken earlier in the fall. He looked perfect. He looked alive.

A slideshow was played with pictures of Matt, his family and friends. There were lots of him and me as well. It was strange for me to see pictures of Matt and the life he had had before we were together, but he still looked like the same Matt that I knew in all of them. The song "Candle in the Wind" played in the background, one of Matt's favourites. Tears ran down my face as the pictures flashed on the screen. Speeches followed. Matt's siblings each shared how he had been an incredible role model for them in life. Connor and his dad spoke as well, sharing some funny stories about Matt growing up and being on the baseball field. Then it was open mic, during which a few more people came up to show their respects to Matt. Listening to the stories was the hardest part for me, there were times where I could picture him so clearly that I found it hard to breathe.

I turned to the back of the church and saw Logan. He was wearing all black and sunglasses that hid his eyes. I wanted to go talk to him, but I knew it wasn't a good idea. It pained me to think of Logan. I knew he was the last person to see Matt before he was killed; it made me angry, confused and million other emotions that I didn't know how to process. Seeing Logan's face made me realize that I would really never ever see Matt again. Then the service was over – as fast as it had begun. We were invited to another room for some food. I told Mom I just wanted to go home, that I was tired. So we left. The moment we got into the house, I headed straight for my bed again and collapsed into a hole of darkness.

23.

I stayed in my bed for weeks. I watched old movies and cried often. Mom tried to get me to leave but I refused, saying that she couldn't make me leave. As much as she hated to admit it, she knew I was right. I wasn't eating, either. Mom would bring me food and I would take a few bites or hide it so she would think I had eaten it. I had lots of visitors but refused to see anyone.

This went on for three weeks. By the end of the third week, Mom began to worry and grew impatient with me. She came into my room one morning and opened my blinds.

"What are you doing?" I snapped from my bed.

"You need light," she told me. "Aria, why don't you and I go for a walk? It's a beautiful day outside." I closed my eyes at the sunlight streaming in through the window.

"No thanks." I pulled my blankets back over my head.

Mom walked over to my bed and pulled the sheets away from my face. "Aria, this needs to stop. You're hurting yourself."

"I just want to be alone."

"Sweetheart, you're acting like you're the one who's dead. Matt wouldn't want you to do this to yourself." I began to cry and Mom tried to comfort me.

Matt. Oh, how I longed for Matt. The engulfing smell of his cologne and the contagiousness of his smile. I was starting to forget. I could feel it. The images of him weren't as clear in my mind anymore, and I was so afraid of forgetting him. I wanted his touch again, more than I wanted air to fill my lungs. My life felt meaningless without him. I was incomplete.

Mom got me out of my room for a little while and took me on a walk. We got halfway down the block before I broke down crying, and she took me back home. I took two bites of the turkey sandwich she made me for lunch, and then spent the rest of the day in bed.

That night, Matt came to me in a dream. Although to me it still feels real – I have to tell people it was a dream or they will think I am insane. I opened my eyes and saw him standing at the foot of my bed.

"Aria," he whispered.

"Matt?" I sat up dazed and confused. "What are you doing here?"

"I came to see you." He sat down on the edge of my bed.

"I miss you, Matt," I said. "It hurts so much. Why did you leave me?"

"Oh, babe," he smiled at me. "It will be okay." He paused for a moment before continuing. "Aria, you need to live again. I don't want you to be sad. I want you to live your life. You need to be happy, Aria. You are beautiful when you smile."

I shook my head at his ridiculous comment. "But I want you. I *need* you."

258

"We will be together again," he told me. "All in good time. But right now, I need you to do me a favour."

"What's that?"

"Live!" Matt smiled that beautiful smile at me. "Live for me. Live like you've never lived before. I don't want you to have any regrets, Aria. I love you and I'll love you forever. Always and forever. I'll wait for you."

I smiled. "I love you too." He kissed me lightly on the lips.

Always and forever.

I opened my eyes, and he was gone.

It was early. The sun hadn't even come up yet. I slipped out of bed and went downstairs. I put on a warm pair of boots and sat down on a chair out on the front porch in my pajamas. I wanted to feel something. Anything at all. I felt nothing but emptiness, and I wasn't even sure if that counted as something. I wanted Dad. To feel his arms close tightly around me and tell me it was all going to be okay. It wasn't fair. Nothing seemed fair anymore. I didn't understand why things happened. I stomped my feet hard on the porch and felt something solid that wasn't the ground under one of them.

I looked down and saw a leather-bound Bible underneath my feet. I cringed when I realized I had just stomped on a Bible, unsure if that was some sort of blasphemy. I didn't know what it was doing on the porch. I assumed it was Robert's or Mom's. It wasn't mine, and it definitely wasn't Quinn's. I picked it up and ran my fingers over the cover. I opened it randomly to the book of Job. I peered down and read the first verse I saw. *"And he said, "Naked I came from my mother's womb, and naked shall I return. The LORD gave, and the LORD has taken away; blessed be the name of the LORD."*

I thought about this. I remembered a song we used to sing at church with Dad the words went something like, "You give and take away." I wished it was that simple. Understanding it, I mean. I didn't know if I could ever just accept the fact that we couldn't control what happened to us in life. Why did I get the crap end of the draw?

I don't know how long I had sat outside. Eventually, the sun came up and the front door opened. Robert came out onto the porch. He sat down beside me and was quite for a while.

"What are you reading?" he finally asked, gesturing to the Bible that was still in my hands.

"Nothing." I pressed my lips together and closed the book.

"It's okay to be mad," he said.

"It's not fair."

"No one said it was." Robert's eyes met mine.

"What do you want?" I closed my eyes and leaned back in the chair.

"I want to help you."

I bit my lip. "I don't know if you can."

"I'm willing to give it a shot if you are."

I stared at Robert. I saw a new, gentle persona that I hadn't noticed before. He looked calm and inviting. Safe.

"I just don't get why everyone I love gets taken away from me." My eyes went wide when I realized what I had said.

"My brother died when I was your age," Robert said quietly. I didn't know this, nor why he was telling me this, but I gave him a slight nod.

"I didn't know you had a brother."

"I don't...anymore." I could hear the emotion in his voice. He was opening up, and it wasn't easy for him. "He was killed by a drunk driver."

"I'm sorry." I said the familiar words that people had been saying to me for weeks. The words that I hated.

"It's not your fault he died," Robert shrugged. "I spent about 15 years being angry. I hated the world. I made some poor choices."

"Really?"

"Really," he said. "I got into drugs, got kicked out of my house, got arrested, destroyed my first marriage." I knew Robert had been married once before but Mom never went into detail about it.

"Wow." I didn't know what else to say.

"Then one day," he took a deep breath, "I got tired of being so angry. I had cut off ties with almost everyone in my life. I had no family, no friends, no career; nothing but anger and resentment towards the man that killed Rick."

I was holding back tears. "Why are you telling me this?"

Robert smiled at me. "Because I want you to save yourself from what I went through. I don't want to see you hurt. You need to stop shutting everyone out, Aria. I know it's hard now, but I promise you, it will get easier."

"I don't even know where to start."

"Start with opening up," Robert encouraged. "Tell people how you are feeling. Stop hiding. Stop pretending. Realize that your hurt is there and it's okay. It's okay to be mad, sweetheart; you just need to be real about it."

I thought back to about six months ago, when I would have pulled a shotgun on Robert for calling me sweetheart. I chuckled softly to myself.

"A big part of getting over hurt is learning to trust again," he said. "And that takes time."

"Time," I repeated. The magic word. Matt was all out of time and I had all the time in the world.

"You can do it, Aria. Let yourself heal." He squeezed my hand. "I'm going to make some coffee. Do you want some?"

I looked up at him and a small smile formed across my lips. "Do you even have to ask?"

24.

Over the next month Matt's death was plastered everywhere I went. It was on the news, in the paper and talked about non-stop. Media coverage began to slowly help me understand Matt's last hours before he passed away. I had heard the story at least a hundred times, but now was finally able to fully process it. Connor had told me everything he could remember and his story was still slightly broken up into smaller pieces that didn't make sense.

The boys had been at the school hanging out when a group of guys approached Logan and begun hassling him hard. Words were exchanged and one of the boys threw a punch at Logan. Matt had step forward to intervene and gotten smoked in the head. They said that the second the punch hit Matt, he instantly became brain dead, that there was no chance of survival.

The trial would take place in the summer, but there was a good chance the boys involved would get off easy. No real jail time, maybe a bit of community service if that. They were calling his death an accident. A tragedy for sure, but not attempted murder. It wasn't fair that the two boys would likely get a clean slate while the rest of us got nothing but emptiness in return.

Summer

25.

Matt's trial began three weeks before graduation, but I didn't attend. Callie went and gave me the play-by-play for a while, then I asked her to stop talking about it; it was too painful to relive in my mind. I couldn't keep walking backwards into the past. I needed to heal and move forward.

From what I had learned about Matt's death, he really had just been in the wrong place at the wrong time, but had saved Logan's life by giving up his own. This reminded me of a Bible verse Matt had once quoted as one of his favourites. *"This is how we know what love is: Jesus Christ laid down his life for us. And we ought to lay down our lives for our brothers and sisters."* In my mind, this represented Matt to a T.

Those few months had been hard, but I had survived. I had gone back to school and graduated with the rest of my class. We had a moment of silence at the ceremony when they called Matt's name. His parents and siblings were called up and the school presented them with an honourary diploma. Callie was named class Valedictorian and I – yes, I – had made the honour roll.

The school built a memorial next to the baseball diamond for Matt. On the last day of classes, I cut out early and wandered down to the baseball field. A plaque had been put into the ground in his memory. Pictures and flowers surrounded it. I knelt down in front of the memorial and closed my eyes. I opened them again, realizing someone was standing behind me. I craned my head around and saw Logan standing there, watching me.

He was wearing a pair of cargo shorts, flip flops and a blue polo t-shirt. I had never seen him in normal clothes before. He looked good. I hadn't talked to him at all since the night at Connor's house. I saw him at the commencement ceremonies, but hadn't known what to say

"Hi," Logan said so quietly that I had to strain my ears to hear him.

"Hi." I stood up.

"I wanted to talk to you –"

"You don't have to –"

"I know I don't," he ran his fingers through his jet black hair, "but I want to." I nodded. "I'm really sorry," he continued. "Matt was – well he was my best friend. Maybe not since you've known him but he was the best friend I've ever had, and he was always there for me – even when it killed him." I swallowed hard and took a deep breath, trying to blink back the tears that were rapidly approaching.

"It's not your fault." I took another deep breath. "I don't blame you."

"He died trying to save me," Logan's eyes were watering.

"He loved you," I told him. "Matt cared about you a lot. He knew you would have done the same for him."

"I would have," Logan whispered.

268

"I believe you." I looked over at the memorial. "Blame isn't going to change what happened. It's not going to bring him back."

"Some of the guys – they hate me."

"They'll come around," I told him. "It's just hard. It hurts and when people hurt, they like to have someone to blame."

"I guess."

"When my dad died last year, I blamed my mom for the longest time. I was so angry and I hated her for it. He died of a heart attack."

"This is different though."

"If it hadn't been you, Logan, it would have been someone else."

"I'm sorry I was such an ass." He smiled at me. I had never seen Logan smile before. His smile was beautiful and took up the bottom half of his face. His smile was like Matt's.

"I think there are a few other people you owe that apology to before me."

"Callie." I saw the pain flash across Logan's face as he said her name. "She hates me."

"Do you still love her?" I crossed my arms over my chest.

"I never stopped," he said. "But it's too –"

"It's not too late. She's still here, isn't she?" I watched as a rush of emotions overcame Logan. He looked completely broken.

"She'll never forgive me."

"She's Callie," I smiled. "You just need to woo her a little."

"After everything I've done –" He pressed his hand to his forehead and struggled to speak.

"Okay, so maybe you need to woo her a lot, but you still can. You can still change things."

He didn't say anything for a moment and then took me completely by surprise. Logan took me in his arms and held me tightly. I started to cry. "Thank you, Aria," he whispered into my ear. "Matt loved you so much, and now I know why. Hold onto his love, Aria, and don't be afraid to let that kind of love find you again." His words soothed my aches and pains as we stood together, crying over the loss of a dear, dear friend.

26.

It was hard to believe five months had passed since Matt's death. It was mid-August and I was at the lake with the family for Robert's work barbeque. I wandered away from the party for a bit and found myself sitting at the end of the dock. The lake was beautiful in the summer. The water was calm and crystal clear, surrounded by large cherry blossom trees. I breathed in the fresh, summer air and felt at peace.

It had been a long summer, full of process and progress. Fall was quickly approaching and a lot of changes would be taking place. I was taking a few months off from school and would then join Callie in Montreal in January. For the first half of summer, I had a job coaching kids' basketball camps at the recreation centre. Most of my nights were spend with Quinn in preparation for her wedding, which was quickly approaching. She was a bit obsessive-compulsive when it came to her big day and needed to discuss everything with me at least 12 times before making a decision.

Robert and I were finally progressing. He really helped me begin to work through Matt's death. I met with him and sometimes with Mom twice a week. We had been working through my emotions and I was journaling on the side. It was a challenge. Matt's death was still so fresh in my mind and was a constant pang in my chest. Every day I woke up was another day where I needed to make a decision to live.

Some days were easy; others were rough. I still had days where I would yell and cry and want to rip someone's eyes out, but these days were less frequent now. The pain in my chest was subsiding and my heart felt a little less broken as the days went on. It was all about steps, Robert told me. Some days I felt like I would move 10 steps forward and then the next day go three steps backwards. This was normal. A lot of my anger about Dad's death came into play with my emotions revolving around Matt. I wasn't angry anymore, though. It was freeing to walk around and not feel like I had a flame of rage burning inside me.

I looked out on to the lake at the water and a memory entered my mind. That was the hardest part. The memories. Everything in Jordan Falls was linked to Matt in some way. I saw him everywhere I went. I thought back to one of the first nights Matt and I spent together down here. The bonfire. Him pushing me into the lake. The laughter. Staying out all night. I closed my eyes and relived the moment slowly. I could almost hear his laughter, feel his touch and taste his lips.

"Hey, does this party have free admission?" Quinn's voice broke my thoughts.

I opened my eyes and smiled. Mom and Quinn both sat down on opposite sides of me.

"Whatcha doing?" Quinn asked.

"Just thinking."

"Penny for your thoughts," Mom offered.

"Just remembering a time I was here," I said, not offering up any more information. They both nodded. They understood. I rested my head on Mom's shoulder.

"Baby steps," she whispered in my ear.

"I love you guys," I told them. "You both are amazing and mean the world to me."

"Aw shucks," Quinn laughed. "I'm blushing." She poked me lightly on the arm.

We looked out on to the lake in silence for a few more moments, then Quinn stood up. "Time to get back to the party?"

"Good idea." Mom stood up beside her. "Aria?"

"Be there in a second." I stood up and looked out at the lake one last time. I watched as a light breeze blew over the water. I felt it lightly brush across my arms and around my body in an embrace. I closed my eyes and broke out into a smile. "Matt." I whispered his name and it echoed all around me.

I turned around and ran down the dock towards Mom and Quinn. The breeze carried me as I ran towards them, still smiling.

ACKNOWLEDGEMENTS

Many people have supported me in the writing of this project. Thanks to my family and friends for encouraging me, as well as letting me choose my laptop over them for several months.

My beta readers: Mom, Elya and Kristen for telling me what worked and what didn't in the early, early stages and pushing me to keep writing.

Everyone else who read this project and encouraged me to pursue it, your feedback kept me going.

Clint - thanks for designing me my awesome cover and helping me to bring this story to life.

Todd - thanks for of all your hard work editing – I appreciate all the time you took to answer my endless questions and help my story to flow better. I'm sure you felt like pulling your hair out everytime you had to write "what does her face look like?". I couldn't have finished this without your help.

Curtis – for helping me format over and over again, until it was perfect.

Holly – you rock. Thanks for reviewing the final edits of this project, lifting me up in encouragement and keeping me sane most of the time.

And last but not least, Joel. Thank you for believing in me, patiently waiting for me and sitting next to me while I edited hours on end all of December. And lastly, for showing me that the world really does have some Matt Lawsons in it.